In Praise of "Wake Me Up Inside" by Lee Bice-Matheson

"This portion of a tale of the supernatural connects the world that teens will know and be familiar with to the terrifying concept of ghosts and the unexplained. The appearance of orbs on Paige's photographs is a nice touch of using small details to increase the feelings of suspense."
— C. Harkin, *Editor, Children's Books, Fitzhenry & Whiteside.* *June 2010*

WAKE ME UP INSIDE, is a novel a person of any age can easily relate to. The author draws us into the heroine, Paige Maddison's character with such detail that the reader immediately becomes emotionally involved. I was intrigued from beginning to end during the protagonist's journey full of adventure and mystery. I can't wait to see what is next to come from this detail-oriented writer. Without hesitation, I would recommend this book to those who are young at heart and crave a suspense thriller.
— Katy Slana, Communications Coordinator

Move over James Patterson...there's a new kid in town and she is going to shine! Can't wait for the sequel and the next, and the next (hopefully)!
— Lyn S.

Wake Me Up Inside

PAIGE MADDISON SERIES

by Lee Bice-Matheson

Published by:

FriesenPress

Suite 300 – 852 Fort Street
Victoria, BC, Canada V8W 1H8

www.friesenpress.com

Distributed to the trade by The Ingram Book Company

This animated short novel is dedicated to my best friend, loving, and, supportive husband, Kevin, who encouraged me to pursue a career in writing after many, many hikes along Ontario trails, spinning yarns along the way to ward off bears. And to our wonderful son, Justin, the source of inspiration for my writing, who enjoyed the stories his mother spun from early childhood. It is coming from a place of love for family, and, for those individuals, who lacked a loving, close-knit, family — this series is for you!

The ancient African proverb, "it takes a village to raise a child", applies as well, to writing a book. I would not have the revised edition of *Wake Me Up Inside* at its best, if not for my husband Kevin, who pitched in around the house when needed and tactfully pointed out many grammatical errors; my sister, Lynn, my official editor, who I will always be grateful for — her time, patience, and effort on this project; my sister, Cindy, who thankfully believed in herself enough to draw the lovely sketch of O'Brien Manor and the Estate; Adam Dagenais of Effigy Design for his most auspicious book cover and loan of his angel from New Zealand; Cole Bennett for my author photo which was painful for me, fun for him; and my son, Justin, who I bounced ideas off of, and he ensured the teen conversations in the book were written with authenticity! To the Readers — I truly hope you enjoy this journey of Paige Maddison's and may it provide an escape for you, if only for a few moments.

CHAPTER ONE

It was an amazing feeling to run through the naked forest free of scratches from errant tree branches; to be invincible. I felt free. Glancing down, I thought how strange to be wearing a flowy, pink and white ruffled dress with a high collar. The feeling of running carefree vanished. Without warning my joyful mood transformed into one of desperation. The sound of wild dogs snapping at my heels prompted me to run for my life. There was no one here to save me. My heart raced as my legs grew sore. I struggled to breathe, desperate to survive. So desperate, in fact, I knowingly jumped off the edge of a cliff. Time slowed in free fall: my heart jumped into my throat and my stomach flip-flopped. I kicked all the way down hoping the effort would break my fall and landed on a boy lying still; as stiff as a corpse in a coffin. My fall did not affect him in any way. I immediately rolled off, horrified by what I thought was true. My eyes grew wide, so wide I expected them to pop. Recoiling, I noticed he was dressed in a black suit with a single red rose placed carefully in folded hands upon his chest. Rising slowly, I nervously looked around. There, in the tall grass, stood a little girl with long, blond hair tied back by a blue ribbon. She stared intently at me.

Waking with a start, beads of sweat rolled off my forehead, dripping onto the bed sheets. Clammy, I felt like throwing up. Glancing out through the bedroom window, I guessed it to be after midnight. The brightness of the summer solstice moon created shadows through the maple trees that danced across the bedroom walls, taunting me upon awakening from my most horrific nightmare. I fell back into a troubled sleep until morning.

* *

"Paige, Paige, didn't you hear me?" mom asked, abruptly, shaking me. "You were supposed to be up half an hour ago. What happened to your alarm?"

Warming sunlight poured in through the bedroom window, forcing thoughts of last night's wicked dream to fade.

"Sorry, mom, I guess I didn't hear it?" I responded lazily, rolling towards her, my eyes closed.

I wondered why she was so agitated. Parents! Suddenly, I noticed a putrid smell in the room. It was disgusting! It must be my gym clothes. I shrugged it off making my way into the shower. A vision of the little girl vividly popped into my head; she was a little waif with intense blue eyes and blond hair. Who was she and what did she want? I tried to dismiss her as I dressed hurriedly for school.

Scrambling downstairs, I grabbed my backpack, a pear off the kitchen table, and yelled urgently, "Mom, don't forget to remind dad to meet me after school with Madame Darling." There was no response. Great!

As usual, the search for mom was on. I found her in the main floor laundry room at exactly eight a.m. She turned and smiled and I realized just how pretty she was. Her smile could light up any room. We both had an athletic shape and the kind of curly hair people came up to touch even though it disgusted us. Oddly enough, we both had moles to the right of our mouths. My friends often commented on how much I looked like her. The only difference: she was a girly-girl and I, on the other hand, was a tomboy.

"Oh, he won't forget, dear. Your dad's really looking forward to speaking with the class. Have a great day at school, Paige!" On that note, she turned to finish loading the washer in our newly renovated laundry room. The bay window dad had installed was a bit over the top but he deemed it necessary for re-sale value.

Happy she was distracted; I quickly exited our Tudor style home. I did not want to tell mom about my nightmare or most recent vision, fearing she would analyze me, again.

We lived in Scarborough, Ontario or 'Scarberia' as my mom often called it. 'Scarberia', much like Siberia, or 'sleeping land', translated into 'an un-exciting place to live'. I often teased her that may have been true in her childhood, centuries ago, but not in mine!

Slamming on my headphones, I began to sing along to Evanescence's song, Bring Me To Life — 'how can you see into my eyes like open doors...' The music motivated me to power walk the half a mile to my high school.

Faintly, in the background, I heard my friend shriek, "Hey Paige, wait up! When are ya bouncin' to your Lollipop's place?"

Darn, just when I was set to break my record of nine minutes and eleven seconds.

"Oh, hi Julie," I answered weakly. She had a twisted way with words. "You mean my grandparents'? Next week."

"We're all going to miss you, Paige. Where are we going to chill now?"

"You'll manage. You and the gang could come to visit me in Camlachie," I replied superficially — thinking as long as she came in a pack of friends. "My parents would love that. Well, I suppose when I know grandpa's okay."

"Oh, I almost forgot about that. I feel bad for you guys," Julie responded empathetically. And that response was why Julie and I had become fast friends. I could always count on her for emotional support.

The severity of the situation hit me. It was true. My grandfather had become ill and was now bound to a wheelchair. Apparently, his care was wearing on my grandmother. She had some help, but not enough. Now, we were needed.

"I can't believe it — one more assignment this year and grade eleven's history! Another year and off to university. What a bummer for you to be leaving Toronto with the best schools! Living in 'Hicksville' Ontario is going to be a drag — the closest university is an hour away," Julie teased.

Julie's hazel eyes twitched when she thought she was funny. My mind wandered as she droned on.

"My mom is sad, too. She claims she won't survive without your dad's help," Julie added, gesturing with her hands.

I reassured Julie that dad's replacement was a talented chiropractor and her mom need not worry. Eager to change the subject, I reminded her of dad's presentation to our class in two days.

"Oh, that should be interesting," Julie winked, and then wiggled her eyebrows. "He's so dreamy with those baby blue eyes, blond hair and tanned face...."

"Okay, that was random," I interrupted, rolling my eyes. Just as we reached school, the irritating sound of the bell reminded us of our duties. "Let's get to class, Julie." As much as I appreciated her, I wasn't going to miss dragging my perpetually late friend to everything.

High school was so boring. I could not wait until my last class of the day to receive approval on my final assignment. As I daydreamed about life beyond these confining walls, the kinesiology teacher, Madame Darling, rudely interrupted me.

"Paige, it's three thirty-two — is your dad coming to meet us today?" she commanded, standing beside me, hands on hips.

"He'll be here any minute...," I stammered, feeling stung by her tone and intimidating stance.

As if on cue, dad's six foot two frame filled the doorway. Madame Darling whisked him away as they became engrossed in conversation, making me redundant. Wandering off towards the dark room, a voice startled me.

"Hey, Paige, are you going to have the photos of the football game done in time for Friday's publication?" asked Tom, the editor of our school newspaper.

"Of course, do you doubt my skills as the 'shutter bug'?" I teased.

"I know you'll do a great job, but the team is still not over the deadline you missed. This is the most important issue of all!"

"Point taken, Tom," I replied smiling as he walked away in green plaid pants and lime-green polo shirt. What a fashion statement!

Walking briskly into the dark room — it dawned on me. This was my favourite place to hang out in the school. The equipment never let me down, although it was in rough shape. Developing the football pictures would be a snap. As I started to process them, several transparent balls appeared– one of which was conical in shape like a wizard's hat. They were randomly located through-out the photos, but not in all of them. Curious. It must be a reflection or some dirt on my camera lens. I hung up the pictures for drying and began to clean the lens. A light tap on the door startled me.

"Just a minute — I'm almost done," I shouted, almost dropping the lens.

Another tap on the door! Wow, don't they know the red light means that I am processing pictures and cannot open the door?

"I'll be right there," I barked.

Exiting the room, I killed the red light. As if walking through a cold breeze, the hairs on my arms stood straight up and I shivered. What is going on?

Suddenly, everything appeared in slow motion — the little girl from my dream was walking towards me down the hall. I became paralyzed with fear in reaction to the physical manifestation in front of me. Unable to move, my eyes rolled slowly towards her trying to make sense of the situation. I realized she held something in her hands that was beyond interpretation. She held my gaze as if to say something and then 'poof' — she disappeared. I flinched as I realized someone was beside me talking to me and snapped back into reality.

"Paige, are you all right?" asked Principal Byrne. "You look pale as a ghost."

"Uh, yeah.... I'm okay. Did you just see a little girl in the hall?" Feeling nauseous, I was almost afraid to hear his answer.

"No. I didn't see anyone else," replied Mr. Byrne. His eyes narrowed as he studied me and with the effect of the pop bottle glasses he wore, his eyes appeared ten times bigger. His shiny, bald head reminded me of a bowling ball, which did not help either. I tried not to giggle.

"Are you sure? She looked ... around eight or nine years old?" I responded indignantly.

"Yes, I'm sure Paige. You're the only one in the hall," he replied, with a puzzled look upon his face.

Like someone hit me in the stomach, I realized how vulnerable and alone I was. Why was this happening to me?

Thankfully, dad appeared. Mr. Byrne nodded at him and walked away. The two men hadn't seen eye to eye on a few issues over the years.

"C'mon, Paige, let's go. I'm finished meeting with Madame Darling," dad commanded with his charming smile.

"Yes, I'm done too," I stammered, slamming my heels on the polished flooring. The pounding of each step resonated through-out the hallway, reflecting my thoughts that time in this institution was drawing to a close. Soon I would be free.

As we burst out the front doors to the parking lot, my dad asked gently, "Paige, are you okay? You don't seem yourself; you're pale, too."

"I'm just hungry, dad," I responded, successfully changing the subject.

"Dinner will be soon. Hang in there, dear."

* * * * * * * * * * * * * * * * * * * *

That night, I lay in bed reading, smelling something faint in the air. It was almost like a newly dug grave — kind of like when you dig a grave for a family pet. My face crinkled as the smell became stronger, burning the insides of my nose. It smelled like dirt from deep down under. The hairs on my arms stood on end, like earlier at school; my heart pounding. What is happening to me? Just then I heard dad clear his throat as he entered the bedroom.

"I am really looking forward to speaking with your class, tomorrow, Paige."

As scared as I was, I quickly recovered and said, "Thanks for donating your time, dad. Madame Darling is thrilled. I know I'm going to get a fantastic grade for bringing you into the class." Imitating Madame Darling walking around the classroom with her nose in the air, I mockingly said, "She feels our generation is so lazy. Chiropractic and the wellness lifestyle teaches us to eat better, think positive thoughts, exercise and sleep enough!"

"Okay, kiddo, that's it," he said, laughing. "See you in the morning."

"Dad?" I sat up.

"What, dear?" His face grew serious.

"Oh, never mind. Goodnight." I lied back down looking interested in my book.   It was evident by the conversation and dad's beaming smile on his small-boned face that he was happy about tomorrow. He was very passionate about his career. I did not want to bother him about weird visions or nightmares tonight.

* *

Sauntering gleefully through the forest, again, in my fancy dress, I felt free; not a worry in the world. It started to rain; the mist was so refreshing. I faced up to the sky, smiling, enjoying the coolness on my skin. Opening my eyes, I looked down at my sleeves and hands and realized the mist was ruby red. I felt sick to my stomach, yet, managed to bolt through the dense brush. The tree branches whipped against my face, cutting my skin. I was in agony. Throwing my arms up to protect myself, I glanced down at pools of blood. My white shoes were now ruby red slippers and I realized, 'I wasn't in Kansas anymore'. Hounds snapped at my heels as I jumped off the edge of the cliff. This time landing on the boy, his eyes opened and I stared into the blackest abyss. My skin crawled; I was petrified. He grabbed me and thorns from the rose ripped into my stomach as he rolled me over, pinning me down, preventing me from drawing a breath.

Mom shook me until I awoke. She was yelling at me.

"Paige, Paige, wake up! Wake up, dear. Kevin, what's wrong with her!?"

"Calm down Lori. Give her a minute."

I slowly opened my eyes and through blurred vision saw my parents' troubled faces. I felt like I had run a marathon. My stomach was on fire, my legs were achy, and my hair was wringing wet. My heart felt like it was going to burst out of my chest. I slowed my breathing, as I gasped, "Dad ... mom... what happened!?"

"Paige, you were thrashing about in your bed and almost fell out. It seemed like you were deathly afraid!" dad exclaimed. "Has this happened to you before?"

Like any smart kid would do, I denied having similar dreams to this one. I did not want my parents putting me under a microscope. Mom left the room to grab a cold cloth for me. She was always nurturing. Dad looked very concerned, apparent by his furrowed brows and rigid frown.

"I knew this move was not agreeing with you, Paige. I'm so sorry we have to go. We're worried about how it's going to affect you."

"Dad, mom doesn't have much of a choice. Grandpa's sick. Mom can't drive to Camlachie and back every day. It's two and a half hours one way. I'm trying to understand," I replied, not believing my own words.

Mom stormed into the room and heard us talking. She placed the cold cloth gently on my forehead, nudging my dad farther down the bedside, and began to speak slowly.

"You know I have to go. I feel terrible making you guys move."

"This was a family decision. We're all in this together, Lori. Right, Paige?"

"Right, dad."

Mom started to cry.

Dad threw his arms around her. I was aware once more of the love they held for each other. They had each married their best friend. I just hoped I would be as lucky one day. My parents turned and hugged me on my oversized double bed. We all cried for a moment and then I tried to assure them that the move was cool. I am not certain I was that convincing, but they did wander off to their bedroom.

Dreams seemed to rule my life, lately. They weren't the kind about butterflies dancing lazily in the garden or sunshine over a beautiful floral meadow. My dreams were not dreams at all. They were nightmares. I glanced at my alarm clock; it was flashing four a.m. Alone in the bed and wide awake, I wondered, what will this move bring?

CHAPTER TWO

"Hey, girlfriend, what's up?! Moving to a bigger place?" asked Geraldo, one of the moving guys. His ironed-on name tag was faded as if washed a zillion times.

"We're moving to a small southwestern hick-town filled with beer-guzzling country folk. It's really going to be fun!" I said, sarcastically, as I trucked another box to our vamped up, super slick, black Dodge Charger with the undersized trunk.

Geraldo brushed past me — what a creep! Moving day was a real thrill.

Realizing I wasn't up for this move, I wondered why should I be? I was leaving the only place I've ever known, and for what?

Finally, my parents came out of the house with the last two boxes. We jumped into the car, which mom often referred to as dad's 'mid-life crisis ride'. It reminded me of a mini hearse, the kind of vehicle for transporting dead people. Now that's a lovely thought! I made myself comfortable on the pillows in the back seat. As we backed out of the driveway, I stared at our house and my chest grew tight — maybe we should be staying right where we are?

"How do you like your new Sirius satellite radio, Paige?" mom inquired, sweetly.

Dad glared as he looked into the rear view mirror and added, "It's from both of us, dear."

"It's great, I love it!" I exclaimed. My thoughts raced. Personally, it felt like a bribe to help me cope with the move. I put my headphones on to calm my thoughts. My favourite song was playing called Ridin by Chamillionaire. In the background, I could faintly hear mom talking to me, but I ignored her until she finally gave up.

"Kevin, I have a bad feeling about this move," mom whispered.

"Lori, you need to go and help with your dad. There's no one else to do it. It could be a little uncomfortable at first; we've hardly spoken to your parents in years. Paige probably doesn't even remember them. When was the last time she saw Ted and Helen?"

"She was probably nine or ten. That's about the time when I had the falling out with dad. I have a bad feeling about this."

"Lori, come on now. You would never forgive yourself if something happened and you weren't there to help. It's time for reconciliation, don't you think?"

"You might be right."

Things grew silent in the car and I wondered what mom was talking about. I didn't know **she** had the falling out with grandpa. Little did my parents know, I was calling my grandparents once a month on my cell phone. I found their number in mom's Blackberry and when I called, they asked me to keep it a secret from my parents. Surely there was no harm in that?

Hours seemed to drag on. After wiggling about to get comfortable, I fell into a deep sleep evident by the drool on my pillow upon awakening. I quickly wiped it off. As I sat up, a most beautiful forest, full of maple, oak and cedar trees, appearing hundreds of years old, came into view. Was that a deer? Could it be? Just as I was about to tell my parents, I spied the most magnificent mansion. It seemed to tower high above the forest. A stone archway with the engraved words 'O'Brien Manor' loomed, as we rounded a curve on the unpaved road. My heart skipped a beat as I ripped my headphones off.

"Mom, isn't that your maiden name, O'Brien?" I asked, astonished.

"Yes it is. This is where we're going to be living for the next while," mom affirmed as she turned to look at me, frantically twirling her hair.

Her voice was shaky. It was obvious she was not happy to be here. However, it was the coolest place I had ever seen! Maybe things would be better than I thought at O'Brien Manor?

We drove down a long and winding, bumpy, cobblestone road that eventually ended up at the Manor. Dad babbled on about how wonderful this place was. Closing my eyes, I wanted to remember this moment for the rest of my life. I had no idea we were from money. I mean, clearly, we must have been. As we exited the car, an older, plumpish woman appeared in the front doorway. Her high-pitched voice sounded familiar.

"Well, Miss Lori, can I help you with your bags? It's so good to see you. Your parents will be so happy to see all of you." She ran over and hugged mom awkwardly in the midst of mom picking up her luggage. Then she turned and said with delight, "Welcome, Paige, Kevin."

"No, we can handle our bags, but thanks for the offer. It's so good to see you, too. Are my folks inside?" mom asked, insistently, while pulling a piece of luggage, almost as tall as she was. It looked hilarious but I tried to hide my laughter!

"No, dear, they're in town for the afternoon at a doctor's appointment. It couldn't wait. C'mon in, and I'll make you a cup of tea and some lemonade for Paige." Hanna stared at me, thoughtfully.

"That would be great, Hanna. Where shall we put our bags?" mom ping- ponged back.

"I hate to be the one to tell you this, Miss Lori, but your dad is insisting that you stay in the guest house. You know where that is — through the back of the Manor and along the garden path?"

"Are you kidding me, Hanna? No one has stayed in that house for years!" mom exclaimed.

Hanna paused inside the massive double doors. "Your dad had it fixed up just for you and your family. You'll find the two bedrooms on the main floor all set up and the kitchen has some new appliances and some other things. You'll see."

"I'm not so sure about this, Hanna," mom said as she frowned, spilling inside the Manor, luggage and all. "How can I help mom look after dad if I'm staying so far away? Besides, that place used to scare me half to death! I shouldn't be so surprised by all of this!"

"Now Lori, maybe it's best this way," dad said cheerily as he walked up behind mom and rubbed her shoulders. "We can have our own family time at night and you can help your mom during the day. It'll be okay. Thanks, Hanna."

I thought it was odd we were staying in the guest house, but I didn't care where we slept. I was so taken in by this monstrosity that mom at one time called home. She had mentioned a few things about it, but never that it was enormous.

"Mom, how many rooms does this place have?" I asked as we stood inside the over-sized wooden doors. Craning my neck trying to view the upper landing, I added, "I could fit my entire school in here."

"There are exactly sixty-two rooms, although dad'll say there's sixty-three. He doesn't know what he's talking about. I counted them all when I was about your age. Let's get our bags to the guest house and put our feet up for awhile. Then we'll have tea, Hanna."

As mom spoke, a chill came over me. It was so cold — shivering, I broke out into goosebumps all over. Judging by mom, she seemed to be experiencing the same thing as evident by the frightened look on her face. She glared at me so I said nothing to dad. What was happening?

We walked through the front 'foyer', a word I had never heard before until Hanna used it on our official tour. It was beautiful! I saw white marble floors and a huge staircase made of a rare, black walnut wood. It was located in the center of the Manor and led to the second floor, its width triple any staircase I had ever seen. There was a wall to wall landing on the second floor; a place I felt curiously drawn to.

As we entered the dining room, I thought I saw something move out of the corner of my eye, over on the staircase. My heart stopped for a moment. The hairs on my arms stood up, like someone waved something electrically charged over them, and a chill ran through my body once again. I must be going crazy.

We all walked quietly through the Manor and out to the back gardens, leaving Hanna behind to prepare for the night's 'feast' as she called it. I was so relieved to be outside! Patches of purple and yellow pansies swayed in the breeze, on either side of the path to the guest house. The grandfather trees ahead bowed as if welcoming us to our new home. Gasping, I saw a stream up ahead with a stone bridge across it. It was an awesome site! Soon after, our guest house towered above us. It was made of flagstone with a turret as our entry point, two storeys high. There were beautifully arched windows on either side of the upper floor balcony. It reminded me of a castle.

Crossing the threshold into our new home, all three of us stopped abruptly to look up at the mural-covered ceiling. Angels carried harps amidst the clouds. When the sun shone in through the windows, the light seemed to bounce off the waxed marble floors to the ceiling and created the illusion of angels actually flying.

"Well then," dad stammered, "your dad went to a lot of trouble for us. Has it always looked like this, Lori?"

"No, no, I don't remember it. They are here protecting us," mom said under her breath, eyes glued to the ceiling.

"What did you say, Mom?" I asked, observing the haunted look upon her face.

"Oh... nothing, Paige. I'm just muttering." Mom did not stray from staring at the ceiling. It was troubling to see her like that.

"It's magnificent!" I cried trying to change the mood. "The ceiling, I mean."

We explored our new digs. It was brightly lit with big windows channeling the sunlight through-out the living areas: the kitchen was on my right as I walked through the front door, with an archway leading into the dining room. It was also accessible from the hallway with a large sitting area across the way. The kitchen had all the latest appliances — blender, bagel toaster, stainless steel fridge with ice-maker and matching microwave oven. The dining room housed a twelve person cherry wood table and chairs, as well as the biggest china cabinet I had ever seen. Continuing down the massive hallway was the master bedroom and ensuite on the left, and my bedroom with walk-in closet on the right. How cool was that?

"Looks like I'll be sharing your bathroom, mom... and dad."

"Oh, we'll have to look into another option for you, Paige. You take way too long in the shower," retorted dad.

We all laughed.

"Hey, Lori, Ted made sure you could still write for the magazine. Look at the computer desk in the sitting room! You'll be able to lay out all your research books and your laptop. That was nice!" my dad exclaimed. "Lori?"

Mom was sitting on a red velvet loveseat located farther down the hall, crying. Dad sprinted to her and sat down, gently wrapping his arm around her shoulders. "Lori, what's the matter?" he asked quietly.

"I'm just a bit overwhelmed. I always think the worst of my dad, but look at all the trouble he's gone to. It must have cost him a fortune. They didn't need this worry while he's so sick."

Mom stopped talking and looked startled as a man marched through the back entrance and right into the house.

"Oh, don't worry about it, Mrs. Maddison. I did the renovations myself and really enjoyed doing it. I didn't take their money and run. Your parents are like my own. My name is Dexter — nice to meet you folks! I live just about a mile to the west."

Dexter reached out to shake hands and winked at me as I approached. I noticed his Scottish brogue right away. He was handsome in a rugged kind of manner, with blond hair, green eyes, goatee, and a tattoo on his upper right arm. It looked like a religious symbol. I'd have to ask him about it later, if we see more of him. I noticed dad was a bit cool to Dexter which seemed strange. New surroundings, new people; maybe everyone was a bit off today?

"We can't thank you enough. You did a great job — did you paint the ceiling as well?" inquired mom.

"As much as I'd like to take credit for it, no ma'am. We found it under the wall-paper on the ceiling... which was odd in itself. The day we discovered it was a big surprise, even to your parents. But...

then… there are a lot of mysteries around this ole estate, aren't there?" he said as he winked. Dexter looked directly at mom.

"Umm, yes, I guess so," she said softly.

"If you need any help, any handy work done, I'm here and I'll leave my card on the kitchen counter — it has my cell phone number. Take care, folks. Nice meeting you all."

Dexter left as swiftly as he had arrived. It was obvious he was familiar with this estate, as he bolted out the front door. Today had been one emotional day, and we were yet to meet my grandparents.

The piercing ring of the phone ricocheted through my body. It belonged to an antique phone with brass handset, seated high on a brass holder. How old is this place? Hanna wished to let us know our tea and lemonade were ready. We meandered back to the Manor. I counted one thousand, one hundred and forty-two steps. Hanna met us at the kitchen door.

"Your folks will be here any time now, Lori. They'll be so glad to see you all. C'mon and let's sit down in the drawing room. It's your dad's favourite place now."

"Thank you, Hanna," mom said warmly. Finally, she was starting to relax!

The three of us settled in on an extremely long and formal couch while Hanna chose a winged-back chair opposite to us. I studied her pale, round face and tired eyes; her greying hair tied back in a bun. She wore a floral dress with a polka dotted apron oblivious to the fashion faux pas of clashing prints. More importantly, she had a gentle, caring manner about her. My thoughts were interrupted by a loud bang at the front door and my grandpa's booming voice.

"Where's my daughter?" he bellowed. It's been seven years since I've seen you, Lori. Where are you?"

Hesitantly, I meandered into the foyer; there was my grandpa in a wheelchair. He was a big man with thick, white hair and beard. His eyes were huge, chestnut brown in colour, contrasting starkly against his rusty complexion. He gazed upon mom with pure love. Whatever falling out they'd had, grandpa appeared over it.

"Hi, dad! It is so great to see you both," she replied, nodding as grandma entered the doorway.

Mom leaned down, hugging him as grandma turned to me, announcing, "And you must be Paige. It's been so long since we've seen you, dear. My goodness, you look just like your mother did at your age. You have your mom's beautiful, brown eyes and long, curly, auburn hair. I also see the two of you are the same height — five foot nothing." She paused, and chuckled. "And — you're so lucky you inherited your mom's delicate nose."

I did not know what to say to that, so I smiled. She nodded at my dad as he, too, entered the room. After several awkward moments, Hanna ushered us into the drawing room to finish our tea and lemonade. The adults settled down to catch up on each other's lives while I wandered off into the foyer. I could not stop wondering what was upstairs. Slowly ascending the staircase, I felt anxious expecting to see something. Instinctively, I moved quietly, without understanding why. The floral carvings on the banisters were remarkable and my fingers traced along each one. As I approached the landing, the air turned ice cold — as if walking into a butcher's meat locker. I thought I could see my breath but knew that would be impossible. My obsessive compulsive nature urged me to continue and follow the railing around to the right. I sensed a hidden panel or section of panels in the wall, although invisible to the naked eye. Just as I was about to explore further, footsteps sounded on the stairs and I felt a slight tap on my left shoulder. Turning around, there was no one there?! Scared out of my mind, I ran down the stairs, two at a time, and back into the drawing room.

"What's the matter, dear?" demanded dad. "You look like you've seen a ghost."

"It's nothing, nothing at all," I gasped. "I just tripped on the stairs." I lied, feeling panicked.

"My dear, Paige, we don't want you to ever go up there. We don't want anyone to," quipped my grandmother. "I hope you understand; the staircase hasn't been used in years. We're not quite sure how safe it is and we wouldn't want anyone to hurt themselves."

"Okay, mom. You understand, don't you, Paige?" interjected mom.

"Yes, grandma, I'll stick to the main floor, don't worry. Think I'll go lie down now, though, if you don't mind. It's been quite a day." Fidgeting on my feet, I couldn't wait to escape the Manor.

"I guess it's not just us old-timers that need a nap," grandpa teased. "Your grandmother and I will catch up with you at dinner, Paige."

"Okay, dear. Are you alright?" mom asked as she approached me. "Do you know your way back, or should dad walk you there?"

"No, mom, I know the way. I'm fine. See you before dinner." I lied, again. Although it was exciting in these new surroundings, I felt disturbed and hoped the fresh air would help.

I kissed my parents good-bye and hugged my grandparents. What in the world had gone so wrong between them? Hurrying through the drawing room, the dining room and kitchen, out the back door to our 'house', my mind raced. It was so bizarre. Who would have thought we would be living at a mansion ten times bigger than our home in Toronto, with a guest house! They were ginormous.

For a moment, I forgot how scared I was and began appreciating the forest around me. The sound of the babbling stream ahead calmed me as did the wind whispering through the trees. If I didn't know any better, it was as if they were actually talking to me! I could not have imagined the beauty of this place if I had not seen it for myself. The tranquility was broken when the bushes near the bridge suddenly moved. I jumped. A low guttural grunt scared the life out of me as a guy my age leapt from the bushes.

"Hi there, didn't mean to scare you. My name is Brad — Bradley Adam Parkman, to be exact, or Baps for short if you like. That's what my mom calls me. Sorry, am I babbling?"

"Why, what were you thinking? You scared me half to death. Do you do that often? I mean hide in the bushes and wait for unsuspecting people to walk by?" I fumed, but happy to have relieved some of my tension.

"My mom told me that you and your family were moving back here to Camlachie, to O'Brien Manor. I didn't believe her and walked over from our property, just east of here. I was walking along the path when I heard someone coming. To tell you the truth, I find these woods rather creepy. You must be Paige?"

"Sorry –yes, I'm Paige. Think I'll stick with Brad. And what's a big guy like you so afraid of in the forest? It's so peaceful here."

"I know it sounds kinda stupid, but wait, you'll see. A couple of weeks here and you'll start — uhmmm...noticing things," Brad said reluctantly.

"O...kaay. So you're Brad. My grandma has mentioned you a couple of times. What can you tell me about my grandparents? I hardly know anything about them."

"I'm the errand boy since they're getting... older. They didn't have anyone else to help them 'til now. I buy their groceries and get their prescriptions filled. Hanna seems to have her hands full with the cleaning and care giving for your grandfather. It hasn't been easy on any of them."

"I know it hasn't. For some reason, it's not so easy on my mom coming back here either. Everything is a mystery and it's really starting to bug me. And you just dodged my question, right now, about what you know of my grandparents! Look, I'm heading to our guest house. Do you want to come along and have something to drink? Then we can talk and get out of this heat." I pushed past Brad expecting him to follow.

"Are you sure it's all right?" he hesitated, standing still like a statue.

"I'm more than sure. All I've seen are adults. It's nice to meet someone without grey hairs. C'mon." I gestured for him to join me.

We walked on the path, one behind the other. Brad took the lead and as I watched him carefully hold back a nasty tree branch for me, I thought how lucky my grandparents were to have someone like this to help them.

Brad had a pockmarked face and shaggy, brown hair to his shoulders, with dark brown eyes, so dark they almost looked black. His face lit up when he smiled — Brad was really handsome. He was tall and walked with confidence — most of the guys I knew had poor posture. His faded jean jacket looked a thousand years old, probably his favourite, and his jeans, ripped, the way teens wore them. It was too hot to be wearing long pants, though. The trip to the guest house seemed quick.

"After you," Brad said graciously opening the front door for me. "Thanks for asking me over. I've never seen the inside of this place and always wanted to. Tried to peek in through the curtains but they were always shut. I wasn't allowed in here when the construction was going on, either. Wow, look at the ceiling! It's magnificent!" Brad exclaimed, waving his arms about.

Interesting — that's the same word I used when I saw the ceiling. Great minds think alike. "I'll get you that drink — Coke or Mountain Dew?" I smiled at Brad.

"Dew, thanks. What do you know about your grandparents, Paige?"

I passed Brad his drink and motioned for him to follow me into the dining room. "Have a seat. Like I said, not much."

"Well, I know that you spoke to your grandparents on the phone. They were so pleased. I always knew when they had talked to you — your grandmother would bake her famous buttery shortbreads and share some of your stories with me. But did they tell you much about themselves?"

"Awkward! What stories? Actually, come to think of it, they didn't. They both had a way of asking what we were all up to. I wanted to keep the conversations short so the call wouldn't stand out on the cell phone bill."

"Your grandma, or Mrs. O as I call her, loved to tell me about your tennis matches. Also — that you were the school photographer. But back to your grandparents — your grandfather inherited this estate. I know he's lived here most of his life. He met your grandmother while he was on a trip with his parents, back home to Scotland. Your Grandma's pretty well lost most of her accent, but once in a while when she's excited, it comes back. And look out when that happens." Brad laughed.

My face flushed — "I've learned more about my grandparents from you in five minutes than from my own parents. Thank you for that. Anything else?"

"My mom told me to keep a few secrets about the O'Brien's. It's all hearsay. I do know she won't step into the Manor for whatever reasons. Whenever I mention I've been inside, she gets a strange look on her face. What's up with the adults around here, eh? They keep so many secrets. Maybe we should change the subject."

"Okay," I said begrudgingly. Brad's posture changed indicating to me he was uncomfortable talking so much about my grandparents. He told me more than I'd ever heard from my parents and I didn't want to push him any further at this point. "So, what do you do for fun in the summer? Isn't it great school's out? One more year, and then off to university," I blurted out. Now I seemed to be babbling.

"I just graduated... grade twelve. I'm helping my mom with her quilting store in town. It's popular with the folks around here. We're designing a website to go global. She'll be able to export around the world. That's what I do for fun."

I marvelled as Brad described his life. His eyes lit up when he talked about marketing his mom's store. He must be close to her or surely he would be long gone from here. Maybe there's more to this country bumpkin place than I thought?

CHAPTER THREE

As Brad and I chatty-cathied about our experiences at high school, I found myself distracted by the sound of footsteps overhead. I realized he could not hear them, or Brad would have stopped talking. Curious, I let him go on about how lame some of the kids around here were. What a pleasure it was to have someone to talk to without wrinkles. The sound of footsteps pacing back and forth troubled me. It sounded so real.

"Paige, are you all right? Your face is white. What's wrong?" asked Brad, urgently.

"Can't you hear that? It sounds like someone's upstairs!" I snapped back.

"No, Paige, but if you'd like, I can go see what it is?" He smiled reassuringly.

"Thanks, Brad. I'm afraid to move." I was beginning to loathe myself for feeling helpless, lately. That would have to change.

"Don't worry, Paige. I'll be right back." Brad dashed from the dining room.

Listening intently, I felt frustrated that I could not hear him for a few minutes; it felt like hours. Finally, he bellowed, "It's all right, Paige. C'mon up. Dexter's here fixing something."

Dexter?! When did he come in?

Hesitantly climbing the stairs to the second floor, I felt panicked. My vision blurred briefly, as I reached the second floor, and became distorted as if there were dozens upon dozens of rooms. That was not possible. After rubbing my eyes, my focus returned and I counted four rooms on either side of the hallway. The male voices directed my steps and there was Dexter and Brad in the second room on the left.

"Hello, again, Paige. I forgot to fix a tap in here. I figured since there are three of you, another bathroom might come in handy. Didn't mean to scare you! Next time, I'll let you know when I'm coming. It's a bad habit — I've been able to come and go as I please in this house while fixing her up."

"It's okay, I guess. But, yeah, you should have let us know! My mom and dad cherish their privacy." I knew I would not be coming up here to use this bathroom by myself. Too creepy!

"I'll be done in a minute and out of your way." Dexter seemed unconcerned.

"Let's go back to the board room, I mean dining room table, Paige," Brad suggested, trying to lighten the mood. "I couldn't believe how scared you were?! Is everything all right?" he pressed, as we scrambled downstairs side by side.

I began to tell the tale of the past week: about the nightmares before I moved here, my experience outside the dark room at my old school, the feeling I had when I first entered the Manor and later, the fright on the staircase. Brad's eyes widened as he listened. He looked frightened. I concluded that must be a bad thing considering he and his mother knew more about this place than I did. Sensing he was holding something back from me, I felt vulnerable and I did not like it. However, it was a relief to finally share my experiences with a friend. Even though I had just met Brad, I felt I could trust him. It felt fantabulous!

"Paige, I'm all done. Are you kids, okay?" asked Dexter, as he caught up with us in our new chillin' spot in the dining room.

"As long as you don't do that again!" I replied half-heartedly, nodding my head. "I mean you might wake up the dead around here, or something!"

"Sure thing. I'll see myself out. Sorry for the fright!" Dexter gave me a funny look and waved good-bye to us. The front door slammed shut.

Brad sat across from me at the mammoth antique table. He turned his soulful eyes upon me. Although, it felt like he was a million miles out of reach, I was in heaven.

"Paige, we need to talk... but I can't right now. I have to help out at my mom's store. Call you later, okay?"

"Sure, Brad." I grabbed Brad's Blackberry from the table and punched in my number. "Call me on my cell, or text." I handed his phone back and lingered as I touched his hand.

"Great, Paige. Talk… later."

Brad's face flushed and he left rather quickly. That was interesting. But, his pensive mood bothered me. That and the fact, that every time we were ready to talk about something real, he changed the subject or had to leave. Well — I could not avoid my family any longer, and headed back up to the Manor.

The walk cheered me as I dismissed what had happened. Approaching the back of the Manor, I scrutinized the second storey windows. The sun reflected so brightly off them; for a moment, I thought I saw something. Paige, quit scaring yourself! This time, I counted one thousand, one hundred and fifty-two steps upon entering through the screened kitchen door.

"Oh good, Paige, you're back," greeted Hanna as she stood by her post at the sink. "Can I get you anything?"

"Yes, I would love some lemonade … if there's any left?"

While Hanna poured a glass for me, I glanced around the kitchen. It was huge, with lots of windows and plenty of counter space. It had sky blue walls and white cabinets with a navy and white speckled countertop. Quite striking, really! And a cosy breakfast nook, too.

"Hanna, did my grandparents have big parties here? I notice tables for twelve, everywhere."

"Yes, back in the day. There were plenty of parties — fundraisers for charity.

Your grandparents raised enough money to start a private school. They eventually sold it for a profit. They have a lot of varied…" Hanna's already high-pitch voice went up an octave as she looked past me.

"Maybe you should leave the divulging of our interests to us, Hanna," grandma quipped as she entered the kitchen. "Could you please go now and check on Ted's blood pressure? He's looking a bit red in the face. We don't want another spell. Thank you, Hanna."

"Certainly, ma'am." Hanna looked at me wistfully, and then left the room.

"Paige, if you want to know anything about us, just ask dear. Don't pay attention to the gossip around here. Some folks like to make things larger than life," Grandma said scornfully.

"I'm just a bit mystified about this huge Manor and your property. I didn't know you…well, you're rich?"

Grandma laughed. "I know it looks that way, but the estate was handed down to your grandfather from his father, and his father before him. There is a trust for repairs. But, we've had to work hard to keep all of this going."

I was about to learn more about my ancestors, when mom's arrival sharply changed the mood.

"Paige, don't bother your grandma about all of this right now. The two of you have just been reunited. You probably barely remember my mom, or dad," she smirked.

Oh, oh. Now, I was in trouble. I started to sweat.

"Well dear, you had better tell your mom about our little secret," grandma slyly suggested.

"What secret, Paige?" asked mom, as she looked deeply into my eyes.

"Grandma, that's not fair," I protested, trying to deflect answering the question.

"Paige, what are you two talking about?" demanded mom.

"Okaay. I called grandma and grandpa once a month on my cell phone. I didn't want to hurt your feelings, mom. " I lowered my head.

She laughed. Her grandiose smile revealed she knew my secret all along.

"Now, don't you think I noticed the number on our cell phone bill? I've known from the beginning. I thought it was great you kept in touch but I did wonder for awhile when were you going to tell me, Paige? Since you never did, I wonder what other secrets have you kept from your father and I?"

"Secrets, it seems like you're the one keeping a lot of secrets," I said, accusingly.

"Yes, dear, I can see how you might think that. We all need to get re-acquainted, then everything will fall into place," mom replied, softly.

Grandma walked over, and put her arm around mom's waist. They both smiled and motioned for me to come over for a hug. I could see that there was love between them; hopefully all three of them. And in that inspirational moment, hope snuck in. I looked forward to discovering O'Brien Manor and the secrets of my family's past.

CHAPTER FOUR

"Dinner's ready! C'mon everyone. We're having a feast tonight! I cooked a turkey with cranberry stuffing, mashed potatoes with my famous gravy, and the best peaches and cream corn you'll every taste. And let's not forget about my fabulous roast beef and Yorkshire pudding! Hurry up before it gets cold!" cried Hanna.

"We're coming," grandma curtly replied.

I watched as grandma pushed grandpa from the drawing room to the dining room table. Why didn't grandpa wheel himself to the table? Maybe he's sicker than he appears? My dad sat opposite grandpa, both at the heads of the table, with mom and I seated across from grandma and an empty place setting. Interesting!

"I've invited Bradley here for dinner tonight, but he may be a few minutes late," stated grandma. Her steely look melted and she winked at me and smiled.

I felt butterflies in my stomach and thought that was unnecessary. I mean, I'm not attracted to Brad, am I? I couldn't be! Later!

There was a loud knock at the front door and into the dining room strutted Brad. I immediately became flushed.

"Hey there, pretty lady," Brad said to grandma. "I've brought some flowers for you and your guests." Brad turned and smiled at me, revealing previously unnoticed dimples. Check!

I was completely enamoured with his looks and personality. I had never felt like this before! It must be the new surroundings. I loved how he treated the adults. All through dinner there was interesting conversation. Brad talked about what it was like to live in a small town, close to the lake, and work with his mom. I could see my parents warming up to him. However, grandpa remained quiet all through dinner. Then it hit me. Grandma invited Brad to ensure there were no uncomfortable gaps of silence or harsh words exchanged tonight. I could see mom stiffen up as she noticed her dad staring intently at her through-out the entire meal.

"Well, Bradley. It sure has been nice having you here for dinner, but if I recall, you have an early morning doing some important shopping for me," said grandpa.

"Of course... I must be going. I'll see you at eight a.m. sharp," replied Brad, with that award winning smile of his. "And Paige, I hope to see you sometime tomorrow, too."

"Yup, sure thing," I shot back.

Brad turned and winked at me as he left the room. I was so embarrassed. My face turned beet red.

"Well, I can see you two have an attraction for each other, dear. I thought I'd get it out in the open. I think he's a nice boy," dad commented.

"He is!" agreed grandpa and grandma in unison.

"Well, then, it's unanimous," added mom. "I think he's very nice too, Paige. He'll be a good friend to have here at O'Brien Manor. Remember, just friends." She raised her right eyebrow — that made me crazy. Did I dictate my parents' life?

"Okay, mom, I get it."

I could have died discussing this with everyone. Mental note: I'll have to hide my feelings a little better next time.

"Why did all of you have a falling out?" I retorted. "I mean it looks like you're getting along?"

Grandpa spit out his drink of water while grandma looked on in dismay, as did my mother. Dad smiled.

"Ah, now we can get to the root of the matter, Lori. We might as well get it all out on the table, right Ted?" dad directed to grandpa.

Grandpa looked distant. He started to speak purposefully to the group.

"It's my fault, Paige. Sometimes, fathers think they know what's best for their daughters, better than they do for themselves. I made a mistake. No, let me correct that, I made many mistakes imposing my opinions on your mother when I should have just let her make her own decisions at the time! As one grows older, and for me, well... sitting in a wheelchair, you realize how stubborn you can be and regret certain moments. That moment for me happened when I told your mother she should have more children. We needed a male heir for the Manor and estate. Your folks were happy to have you and completely fulfilled! Now, I can see why. It was stupid of me and I'm sorry," confessed grandpa, looking soulfully at mom.

Mom started to cry, as did grandma. Now I understood the problem.

"I resent that grandpa," I responded. "Why can't I inherit the estate and look after it someday? C'mon, this is the era of liberation. Women do many things that men can do, and more..."

"Please, don't you be mad at me too, Paige. I couldn't bear it," grandpa pleaded.

I ran over to hug him.

"I'm sort of kidding, grandpa. But I love it here. I could come back and live here someday to take care of things. I guess my parents would have to run it in the meantime," I coyly responded.

"This is a pretty deep subject, folks," said dad. "Let's all calm down and relax. We can talk about it again over the next few days, or weeks, for that matter. We're here for awhile."

Mom sat in silence. I felt bad for asking the question but happy to hear that was all there was to it! Now, maybe, there could be some healing in the family.

I jumped as a loud bang sounded from the stairs.

"That must be Mackenzie, our invisible house guest. She's agreeing with you Paige," mocked grandpa, a mischievous look on his face.

"Who's Mackenzie?" I asked. Invisible, what does he mean?

"It's just a joke," murmured grandma as she quickly changed the subject. "You seem to be on edge, Paige. There are lots of sounds you will have to get used to, in an old mansion like this!"

"All right, then! Well I think we should let Ted get some sleep," interrupted dad.

"Not before I respond to what my dad just said," mom retorted. "I've been waiting to hear those words for so long, dad. I can't thank you enough, tonight, for having the honesty and compassion to say it. I forgive you, and I hope you'll forgive me, for the years that I lost touch with both you and mom. I can hardly believe it's been seven years. I lost all that time with you, and I'm going to make up for it, I promise! I guess I was stubborn, too," she admitted, as tears welled up in her eyes.

Grandpa slowly wheeled his way over to mom. They hugged for several minutes until grandma got up from her chair and joined in. I was relieved they had forgiven each other. I could feel some peace in the room — a warmth that perhaps existed all along? It was wonderful to be at O'Brien Manor; or was it? And who was Mackenzie, anyways?

CHAPTER FIVE

Insomnia hit hard that night. So much had happened in one day. Wow, to think mom and her parents had finally forgiven each other, and so quickly! I thought for sure it would take months to happen. The twinkle in my grandparents' eyes, when they looked at each other, revealed their passion. There was so much to discover about them and their past.

Tossing and turning, my thoughts wandered to the noise we heard coming from upstairs and earlier, to the tap I felt on my shoulder. Someone had surely tapped me, or, was it all my imagination? And why did grandpa say it was Mackenzie on the stairs and then act as if nothing was said?

Glancing around the room was like staring into a black cloud. One small window hindered any chance of seeing in the dark, especially on a cloudy night like this one. I ran my fingertips along the cool, satin sheets while picturing the pink, floral wallpaper. Not my first choice, but it was a luxurious room. My feet slipped easily back and forth across the sheets. The goose-down duvet was so very cosy. I felt like a princess in my Queen Anne poster bed. Grateful for mom healing old wounds, I closed my eyes. When I gradually opened them, a solid black image hovered above me. I squeezed my eyes tightly, and then slowly opened them. The image had not dissipated. My breathing grew shallow. Was I seeing things, or losing my mind? As it moved closer, I collapsed into the bed, fearful it was going to touch me. An odour similar to a guy's sweaty scent, mixed with dirt, burned in my nostrils; the image vanished but its' disgusting smell remained. Lovely! What could it be?

Shivering, I dragged the covers over my head. It was bitterly cold in the room; like being locked in a freezer. Paralyzed with fear, all I could do was try to remain calm. I counted from one to ten again and again, silently freaking out, sensing something still there with me. I barely drew a breath. It was at this moment that I desperately missed my old room — at least I could see everything from my bed! It seemed much less complicated in Toronto!

Quietly, I lay there as I heard my door slowly creak open. I thought I was going to faint until I heard mom's voice.

"Is everything okay in here, Paige?" asked mom quizzically. "I thought I heard you call my name?"

"Oh, mom, please come in! I'm so scared!" I whispered, as I threw back the covers and started to cry.

"What's the matter, Paige? Tell me what is going on?"

She sat down gingerly beside me on the bed.

"You felt it when we walked in to the Manor today, mom. I saw the hairs on your arms stand up, like mine. You gave me a look. I've been hearing things and feeling things all day. Just now, I saw something black on the ceiling and it moved close to me, and then disappeared." I threw myself into my mom's arms, shaking. "Just before you walked in my room, the air turned cold. Don't you feel it?" I threw my head back against the pillow and cried.

"No, dear. I don't think the guest house, or the Manor, is properly heated and that's why we have goose bumps. My parents are trying to save on their heating bills. I was going to talk to them about it in the morning. Buildings that are as old as these have lots of noises and I know it can seem pretty creepy. I remember that as a kid growing up here. There's nothing more to it," mom assured me. She gently brushed the tears from my cheeks.

"Really, mom?"

"Yes, dear."

"So that's all it is," I said, almost disappointed.

"Not that I don't love a good mystery! If you find something out, please let me know and I'd love to rub it into my parents and say 'see, I told you so!'" mom said, mischievously.

"All right, I get it. I guess I'm over-reacting."

"That's good, dear. Goodnight and don't let the bed bugs bite."

"You haven't said that to me in years. Not since I was little."

"I guess it's coming home again that brings out the kid in me. Try to bear with me, okay? Get some sleep. I love you, Paige."

"Me, too. Good night, mom."

As she closed the bedroom door, I felt that chill in the room again. As much as I wanted to believe her, I am not so sure I did. Mental note — remember to ask Dexter about the heating in the morning.

* * * * * * * * * * * * * * * * * * *

I awoke to a loud bang and my mom shrieking while my dad chortled shamelessly. I glanced at my alarm clock and groaned. It was seven in the morning.

"Calm down, Lori! I'll trap him and then I'll ask Dexter to come and see if we have a problem with them. I'm sure it's nothing to be concerned about, dear," dad reassured mom.

"Kevin, it's not funny — I can't stand mice! They freak me out and have, ever since I was a kid!" mom said scornfully.

"I'll give him a call," affirmed dad, as his voice trailed off down the hall.

I sat up and hopped out of bed. The floor was icy cold. Maybe mom was right about the heating? I ran to the closet and slipped on my red Crocs — the only option available since my favourite running shoes were still waiting to be unpacked.

My poor mom. She really hated mice. I entered the hall to find her perched on a chair , pointing and screaming helplessly at the scary, little mouse, and was reminded of one of those ancient TV commercials.

"Mom, it's okay. Dad will take care of it. It's just a mouse," I offered.

"Paige, it's never 'just a mouse', it's always lots of mice. Where there's one, there's seven," replied mom. "They must have a nest in the house."

"Okay, Lori. That's enough. I called Dexter and he's calling his friend Fred who's an exterminator to come and inspect the place and get rid of any and all critters. We'll be at the Manor today and by the time we get home tonight, it'll be fine." Dad glanced at me with a mischievous smirk.

"Dexter should have taken care of this before we moved in!" mom snapped back.

"It's all right, mom. We'll have fun with grandma and grandpa. Whoops! I have to hurry and get changed! I'll meet you up at the Manor." I bolted for my room.

"Why, Paige? What's so important?" teased dad. "A young lad, perhaps?"

"Very funny, dad." I ran into the bedroom realizing my face was flushed, again. I have got to stop that!

I put on my favourite baby blue shorts and white t-shirt with the phrase 'Attitude gets you through life' and jogged to the Manor. I loved the path with all of its flowers and shrubs that revealed the old oak and maple trees and a few cedars. I loved studying trees in grade two. It was all so fascinating at that age. I crossed the stone bridge and saw the bush that Brad had jumped out of. I was confident he would not do that again. As I approached the Manor, I noticed a picnic table on the cement patio by the entrance. Hmm, maybe we could start eating outside when it became a bit cooler?

"Hi, Hanna. Great to see you," I said as I stumbled in through the kitchen door.

"Good morning, Paige. Guess who's in the dining room? I think he's starting to take all his meals here, now," giggled Hanna.

"Very funny, Hanna. I'll go and say hi."

"Uh, huh. Have fun," responded Hanna. "I'll bring you in some eggs and bacon and my hash browns. You're gonna love 'em."

"Thanks, Hanna," I yelled from the drawing room.

Upon entering the dining room, I stopped to watch Brad talking to grandpa. He was frowning at Brad. He spoke so quietly that I could not hear what he was saying. Brad's shoulders were slumped — not a good sign!

"Paige, what are you doing standing in the doorway like that?" asked grandma, who had appeared out of nowhere.

"Oh, nothing, grandma. I don't want to interrupt grandpa and Brad."

"It's okay, dear. Let's go in," grandma said, nudging me into the room. "Good morning, gentlemen. Hard at it already, eh?"

Grandpa glared at grandma for a moment, then turned to me and said, "Good morning, Paige. Did you sleep okay?"

"Yes, grandpa. It's a wonderful bedroom. Thanks to both of you for fixing it up. I love it!" I gushed.

"It was a pleasure, wasn't it grandpa?" grandma admitted, grinning ear to ear.

"Of course," he agreed.

"Hi, Paige. Good to see you this morning! You look bright today," said Brad.

"Why thank you, Brad. Good to see you too." I nervously rubbed my earlobe.

"Would you like to go for a ride in to town?" asked Brad.

"Wait a minute," said Hanna, as she walked into the room with my breakfast, "a young lady needs her proteins."

"Bradley, why don't you go ahead this morning," suggested grandpa, "and we'll visit with Paige. It'll give us a chance to get re-acquainted while her parents are handling their little problem at the guest house."

Brad stood up and stared at me with those heavenly brown eyes. A smile formed on his face and the mood lightened. "Okay, Mr. O. See you later, Paige. I'll catch up with you on your cell," he hollered as he left the Manor.

I blushed, again.

"Did my dad call and tell you about the mouse?" I asked my grand-parents, rather amused.

"No, Paige. Bradley bumped into your dad as he was walking by your place. That's how we knew," replied grandpa.

"Were you and Brad having a few words, grandpa?" I asked, hesitantly.

"Oh no, dear. I was explaining that he couldn't use our truck this morning. There seems to be a problem. It won't start. Maybe your dad could look at it later."

"Yes, he's good with cars and things. I'm sure he can fix it," I responded. "What about this breakfast? Looks good," I commented as I dug my fork into the eggs.

"It's a great day ahead, Paige. I listened to the forecast and it looks like the sunshine is here to stay for the next few days," grandma announced cheerily. "You must have brought it with you."

I returned my grandma's smile. Hmm, a positive forecast for the days ahead. So far, all I have felt was an evil chill!

CHAPTER SIX

Mackenzie felt trapped. A rambunctious nature almost led to her discovery by Paige. She was told to hide in the shadows until Conall said it was okay to be seen. But, Mackenzie could not wait to make a new friend! Yes, Paige was a bit older, but, surely she would want to play with dolls and have tea parties. Conall would be jealous. Where was he anyways? He was always disappearing.

"Mackenzie, what were you doing on the stairs? I saw you tap Paige on the shoulder. Lucky for you she got scared and ran into the drawing room. It's not the right time to meet Paige. You've got to settle down," commanded Conall.

Conall was an overbearing brother. He was not one to understand the need for a friend and certainly wasn't empathetic to anybody but himself. They had lived a lifetime together, it seemed, and Mackenzie was growing tired of his moods. Conall was a brooding, dark soul. He watched and scoffed at the new family that had moved into the guest house. He thought it was particularly funny about the mice on their main floor. Mackenzie, on the other hand, felt sorry for the mother who was apparently quite afraid. She reminded Mackenzie of her own mother. It was the wavy hair and gentle voice in which she often spoke. Who else did she remind her of? Mackenzie thought of her great grandmother.

"Mackenzie, you must stay out of the new people's way," demanded Conall.

"All right!" replied Mackenzie. He never let Mackenzie have any fun. It was beginning to wear on her. "I'll give it a few more days, then I'm

meeting Paige and we are going to play together. I've not had a friend for a very long time!"

Conall vanished as quickly as he had appeared and that bothered Mackenzie. He was becoming so unpredictable. Mackenzie decided to go to the Manor attic to play with her dolls. When she arrived and sat down to sing 'Hush little Baby', she slowly realized someone was watching her from the shadows. It gave her an uneasy feeling.

Sitting in the dusty, old attic was usually comforting for Mackenzie. There were two windows covered in dirt with shutters that barely let in any sunlight. The old, wooden armoire that her mother had used was filled with clothes and Mackenzie would often play dress up and pretend she was the mom in charge. Mackenzie lined up her dolls in a row and decided to play school. There was an old chalkboard and some pink chalk left behind from one of her cousins. Today's lesson would be about geography.

"Now class, pay attention," said Mackenzie. "We have two countries on the board. One is in the shape of a boot and the other is the shape of an animal. Can anybody guess what they're called?"

Mackenzie quieted down as she heard a noise from below. What was that? Is someone coming? She heard distant voices.

* *

"C'mon, Paige, it's all right. I used to come up here when I was a little girl. I never told my mom about it. You have to see the dolls dressed in their fancy little gowns. I believe they were left behind from one of our ancestors. This is exciting! I haven't been up here in years!" exclaimed mom.

Climbing up the narrow, steep stairway was spooky. So, this was the way to the attic. It smelled musty — as if from an era, long ago.

"Are you sure we should be up here, mom?" I asked with great trepidation.

"Yes, dear. Don't worry about it! Grandma and grandpa are lying down. They can't hear us all the way up here," assured mom.

We became silent as mom opened a trap door in the ceiling. I could barely see how to open it. "Wow, mom, you sure know where the secret hiding places are. This is great but I still feel like I'm betraying grandma and grandpa. I really feel guilty," I hesitantly admitted.

"It's okay, Paige. Trust me. We're not hurting anyone. I spent a lot of time rummaging around this old Manor. I didn't have a lot of friends because the closest neighbour back then was over three miles away. I had school friends, but that was it. I had to make my own fun.

I would come up here and play dress-up," mom reminisced. "There's a big mirror too. I hope Dexter hasn't been up here and taken it away."

As I climbed up through the trap door, I lost my breath for a moment. The room was frozen in time. "Mom, did you leave the attic looking like this?"

"I was just thinking about that myself, dear. It looks like someone has re-arranged things. That's odd."

My eyes widened in delight at the beautiful porcelain dolls lined up ever so carefully along the wall. Their dresses were to die for, probably made of taffeta. Two dolls were seated in tiny chairs, a boy and a girl. Their faces were so real. Someone had gone to a lot of trouble to make them look lifelike.

"Mom, whose dolls were they? They're so fragile looking. Can I touch them?"

"Go ahead, Paige. She was my favourite doll," mom explained as she pointed to the blond haired female doll, "and I played with her and the male doll seated next to her a lot. They were like my siblings. I had names for them. Funny, I can't remember them now. That was so long ago. I forgot how authentic they look," mom said as she walked around the room.

I had the feeling that we were not alone. I surveyed the area. Out of the corner of my eye, I saw shadows, but when I looked directly at them, there was nothing there. I had an over-active imagination and it had to stop.

"I love her emerald dress and her ruby necklace. Is it real?"

"Yes, I got it for my tenth birthday and placed it on her. I told my mom I lost it because I wanted her to have it."

"What's her name?"

"Strange... I really can't remember. Oh yeah, and her brother. Wait. Where did he go? Wasn't he just there?" asked mom, quizzically.

I looked around nervously. "I'm not sure. I could've sworn he was. Well, I can see why she was your favourite doll." Goosebumps raged across my body and I suddenly felt very vulnerable.

* *

Mackenzie watched the mother and daughter rather curiously. They seemed to be close. It made her miss her own mother. Mackenzie wanted to meet them so badly but remembered what Conall had said: 'not yet'. Mackenzie's heart sank. When will that time come? She saw Conall grab his doll when the mother and daughters' backs were turned and he

signaled her to leave. He was seething, which was very apparent by the
disgusted look on his face.

* *

"Paige, we should go back downstairs before a search party is sent out for us. We've been missing long enough. Grandpa takes short naps and grandma may have noticed our absence by now."

"Okay, mom," I agreed readily.

We quietly climbed down through the trap door closing it gently behind us and continued down the wickedly narrow staircase. "Good thing we aren't any wider, mom," I said giggling.

"Very funny, Paige. This will be our little secret. Don't tell your dad about it. Sometimes he just can't help but blurt things out. I wanted you to see my secret childhood playground."

When we reached the landing, mom turned and hugged me. She smiled from ear to ear. "I love you so much, Paige. Thank you for coming home with me. It's been so much easier with you here," mom said, tenderly.

I felt my throat tighten as tears filled my eyes. I really didn't want to move to the middle of nowhere but I already felt closer to my mom. She was a lot more fun than I had ever imagined and seemed more youthful here.

"C'mon, mom. You're going to make me cry. My face will swell and I'll turn all red and blotchy," I pleaded, as I gave her the biggest bear hug ever.

"Okay, you almost broke my back. Now, let's get to the main floor. Remember to tread softly."

We barely took a breath as we tippy-toed down the staircase and into the drawing room.

Grandpa bellowed, "Where have you two been?" He was sitting in his wheelchair in the middle of the room, hands outstretched. His face was bright red.

We were speechless, until mom simply declared, "You should be thanking us! We saw a mouse go up the stairs and trapped it and threw it out the window. And they say women cannot handle things like that. I'd say we did a great job. Paige, don't you agree?" mom said as she turned and winked at me.

Grandpa had a sheepish look on his face. "I'm sorry to react like that. It startled me to hear you coming down the stairs. I wasn't sure what was going on?"

"Quite all right, grandpa. We are glad to help." I smiled at mom. *Now we shared a secret!*

CHAPTER SEVEN

A lot had happened since first arriving at the Manor. As much as I wanted to explore every inch of the gothic style manor, it was time to search the grounds. I had no idea what existed beyond our guest house. The past few days, dad was in turmoil settling into his new clinic in town and mom was busy reacquainting herself with my grandparents. Even Bradley Adam Parkman was scarce, helping his mom at her store. Feeling a bit neglected, I had Hanna pack a lunch for me at breakfast and stuffed it in my backpack. After digging through three of the boxes in my bedroom, I finally located my favourite Skechers. Now, I was all set to explore the grounds.

A cobblestone path led into the dense forest from the back door of our 'castle'. It looked like it had not seen any use in years — as if that would ever stop me! The height of the trees ahead was astounding. They must be over a hundred years old! I felt slightly on edge — a semi-permanent state of mine, lately. Vines writhed across a stone archway situated in the middle of the path–it seemed like a warning to visitors. I clawed my way through the gnarly vines, stopping abruptly on the other side — wind whipped through the trees which sounded like someone whistling. I continued along the path and faintly heard water rushing by, but, it was hard to determine where it was coming from. The path ended and now I had to concentrate on the uneven ground before me which consisted of large, jagged rocks. Carefully, I navigated the terrain so as to not accidentally go over on my ankles. Oh, how I hate when that happens!

Engrossed in my present surroundings, I was surprised that a babbling brook popped up in front of me. I narrowly missed falling in! It was beautiful, flowing down from the ridge above. Discovering I needed to cross the brook in order to access the rest of the uncharted Manor grounds, I slowly made my way stepping carefully from stone to stone. I felt foolish as I slipped into the brook, just short of the embankment. My mother's words popped into my mind: 'Be careful to take your shoes off when near the water! You don't want to get a soaker!' Wow!

Frantically grasping onto entangled weeds, I pulled myself up and onto the grass, feeling much like a river rat. While wringing my clothes to dry, I decided to forge ahead up the side of the hill to the ridge, dragging my backpack behind me; it took some time. I had to stop to rest about halfway up, with another thirty to forty feet to go, and, was elated when I reached the top! Standing still overlooking the entire estate — it was breathtaking. The sun shone brightly directly overhead: its reflection bouncing off the surface of the brook, illuminating its flow down the hill, parallel to the guest house and zigzagged towards the Manor. So that's where it leads! Surveying the uncharted part of the estate stood an old, dilapidated building. It looked like a run-down cottage — part of the roof was caved in and the remainder was cloaked in overgrown vines.

Crouching low to grip the stones jutting out of the ground, I stealthily made my way down the steep slope. The rocks provided something to hold on to, preventing me from rolling down to the valley below. One misstep would be fatal, even for the strongest athlete. Perhaps, I should have told someone where I was going today?

I came upon a field brimming with sunflowers and tall grasses. It was such a peaceful setting. However, as I rested for a moment, I noted a dull and constant sound. Then — out of nowhere — bees buzzed all around me. I bolted to the cottage for refuge. Collapsing breathlessly, at a small picnic table, I was relieved to see I had lost the bees; I paused to assess the place. Then, I hesitantly approached and tried the cottage's door handle — it was an antique metal latch, not a doorknob, like I was used to. Of course, the door creaked loudly as it opened, as if to announce my arrival to the long forgotten structure.

It was intriguing! The kitchen had rotting, wooden cupboards and a huge stove that would now be seen only in antique museums — an iron top with a black, matte finish. There was a rectangular dining room table for, what a surprise, twelve. Funny that! Part of the roof had caved in on the hallway, probably where it led to the bedrooms. It looked precarious. I wasn't sure I should go in any further!

The hairs on the back of my neck stood up and it felt as if someone was watching me! I saw something out of the corner of my eye, yet when I looked right or left, it seemed to disappear. This was really getting on my nerves. Creepy, really! Whatever it was, it would not kill my curiosity.

A small library was situated on the other side of the room, across from the dining room table. There were stacks of books covered in dust. I slid my backpack off my shoulder and slipped two random books inside. Turning on my heels, I hastily left the cottage, deciding it was lunch time. I flopped down at the picnic table thinking this must have been some place in its day. While carefully pulling out my egg salad sandwich, I noticed a pile of firewood stacked on the east side of the cottage, and a gardener's shed beyond that. Wow, I really discovered something, today!

Just then, I heard a boy's voice. I spit out my food.

"So you're the new tenant in the Guest House. I wondered when I would meet you? This is my home. What do you think?"

The boy looked about fifteen years old and was wearing a peculiar ruffled shirt and black skinny pants; perhaps goth? He spoke in the same accent as grandma — Scottish, I believe. And no way could he be living here now! This place hadn't been used in a hundred years.

"Where did you come from? And how do you live here? This place is condemned, isn't it?" I queried as I cleaned up my mess.

"Condemned, what do you mean? There is an entrance on the other side to the bedrooms. And the kitchen is still useable. It's lovely. I'm from around here. What's your name?" he asked.

"Paige. And yours?" My gut instinct told me this conversation should not be happening.

"Conall. I hope I didn't surprise you any? I couldn't help but notice how interested you are in this place. There's a lot more to explore on these grounds. Shall I show you?"

He offered his arm assuming I would join him. I ignored him and continued to eat my lunch, responding between bites.

"Uh, no. I don't think so. Do my grandparents know you live here?"

"Your grandfather does. He allows us to live here. I'm not sure about your...umm... grandmother," Conall said slyly.

"Who's us?" I stammered. This whole situation was making me extremely uncomfortable. Why didn't I tell anyone where I was going today?

"My sister, Mackenzie, and I. She really wants to meet you but I told her not yet. She'll be mad at me — that I met you first." He looked coyly at me.

Mackenzie! Where have I heard that name before? Then I remembered. Grandpa made a reference to her — she was on the stairs. "Where is Mackenzie now?" I challenged.

"She's up at the Manor. She loves to watch all of you as you're finding your way around."

"I don't understand. My grandpa never mentioned you." I paused, growing more uneasy. I did not trust Conall. The reference to Mackenzie had been a joke; an invisible friend of my grandparents. "I think I'd better be going."

Quickly packing up my garbage, I rose from the picnic table and speedily walked past Conall. Thinking I had escaped, Conall suddenly appeared before me on the path, blocking my way towards the ridge.

"I really do have to get going, Conall. Please, let me go now," I pleaded.

Conall looked at me with narrowed eyes. They were green and with his burnt orange hair and ruddy complexion; he looked menacing. My knees weakened. Much to my amazement, however, he backed off. Bit by bit, I made my way to the hill. The bees did not capture my attention this time. I was oblivious to my surroundings, distracted by my racing thoughts, knowing I had to tell Brad about this. I finally made it to the top of the ridge and turned around to see where Conall was — he had vanished!

When I started to make my way down towards the brook, I felt a chill as a delicate breeze crossed my body. There on the path below me stood a little girl with long, blond hair dressed in a white, eyelet jumper. It was the little girl from my dreams! My skin crawled. What is going on here today? Wobbling on my feet, I passed out.

I awoke, upside down, my feet above me on the path, remembering I was on a steep slope. I could see the little girl's frightened face. She was kneeling next to me. I sensed she was not the one to fear. Rubbing my head, trying to ignore the pain, I finally found the strength to sit up.

"Are you Paige?" she asked hesitantly, avoiding any eye contact.

"Yes I am," I responded. I did not want to upset her.

"Come on! You have to get up. I'm not the one who will hurt you. I want to talk to you about Conall. Quickly, now, I don't have much time!"

I turned over on my hands and knees and staggered to my feet. Feeling a little dizzy, I carefully slung my backpack over my shoulders and followed her guardedly, down the hill. I did not know what to think.

"My name is Mackenzie. I'm Conall's sister. I wanted to welcome you to the Manor the other day, when you and your mom came up to play with her dolls. I was so excited but didn't want to alarm you."

So Grandpa was telling the truth.

"You were in the attic? I didn't see you. How could that be?" I stammered, nodding and encouraging Mackenzie to go on.

"I was hiding — there's a chamber off the attic and I thought you and your mom wanted to be alone."

"Oh, good thing! My mom doesn't need anything else to upset her right now! She had a run-in with mice in our guest house."

"Yes, I know. We saw it. The handy man should be able to help you out with that problem. He's been around here for years," said Mackenzie, "you know, Dexter."

"Yeah... I need to get back to the Manor now. My family will wonder where I am."

"I'll walk with you," she offered.

"Okay," I readily agreed. Somehow, I was happy to have Mackenzie's company.

We walked together in silence. I made my way successfully across the brook, this time, and along the path, until I saw the stone archway — the portal to the guest house. Something just didn't seem right about meeting my new friends. I was not going to mention it to my parents, just yet, but I needed to talk to Brad right away. As I turned to speak to Mackenzie, she, too, had vanished. This was beginning to freak me out! What is happening to me?

CHAPTER EIGHT

I sprinted to the back entrance of the Guest House, collapsing onto a boulder. My hands were shaking and would not stop. I was not just disturbed about meeting Conall or Mackenzie — what if something had happened during my trek? What if I had sprained my ankle over by the cottage? How would I have gotten home? Who would come to find me? And what if I had fallen over the ridge... I shuddered to think about it and started to cry. I had to gain my composure before talking to my parents. My thoughts were interrupted, suddenly, as I heard a faint noise.

"Ah!" I cried, jerking, and sliding down the boulder, to the unforgiving ground. My nerves were shot. I gradually looked up and there was grandpa, sitting on the boulder I had just fallen from. How on earth could that be?! "Grandpa, what are you doing here?!" I stammered.

"Paige, my dear, you should not be here in the woods! There are things you don't know about, yet, but in time will be revealed to you. Calm down, child. Go back inside the guest house and try to rest before dinner."

Extremely exhausted, I shut my eyes, only to open them, and find grandpa had vanished. That had to be a hallucination! Must be the heat!

I quickly marched straight into the house and flopped on my bed, staring at the ceiling until sleep settled in. The irritating ring of the telephone awoke me. I felt out of sorts and was unsure where I was. Then I remembered and ran for the phone.

"Hello?" I answered, timidly.

"Hi dear, come on up and have some tea with your grandparents, and Dad and I, will you? Where have you been? I called the guest house and your cell several times."

"I was just wandering the grounds a bit, mom. I didn't bring my cell with me. No problem. Sorry to worry you. But mom, I saw Grandpa a few minutes ago, out back, sitting on a boulder."

"What? Paige, are you all right? You don't sound yourself. Grandpa has been here with us all day. How could he even get there? Now, hurry up to the Manor."

Shocked, I hesitated before responding, "Okay, mom. I'll be right there."

I hung up the phone, afraid to venture outside. Afraid? Since when do I get so afraid? Maybe it was a dream? I ran to the back door and opened it just far enough to poke my head out. There on the ground was grandpa's handkerchief, with monogrammed initials T.O. for Ted O'Brien. I felt paralyzed with fear. I must be losing my mind! Dark shadows danced around our backyard as the sun's golden rays streamed through the branches of the trees. The sun had moved to the last quarter of its daily journey. I ran back through the guest house, slammed the front door shut behind me, booting it to the Manor. I arrived dishevelled and upset — not only from the day's experiences, but that I had also forgotten to count the steps to reach the Manor.

"Well, there's our granddaughter!" announced grandpa, as I entered the kitchen. "What have you been doing since breakfast? We missed you around here."

"Oh, just searching the grounds," I muttered, wondering how grandpa could be in two places at once.

"Just be careful, dear," added grandma. "Not all of the grounds are safe! There are paths that haven't been used in years."

"Yeah, I know. I ended up at that old cottage."

Grandpa dropped his cup of tea and barked, "Don't go near there, Paige! It's condemned; not fit for the living. You could get hurt! Promise me you won't go back!"

"All right, then, grandpa. I won't," I agreed as I picked up his tea cup and grabbed a napkin to sop up the mess. "It wasn't a great adventure anyways. I met a strange boy."

"What? Did he tell you where he's from?" demanded grandpa.

"He said he's from around here — Conall, and his sister, Mackenzie."

My grandparents both looked at each other, shocked, quickly recovering.

"Now that's enough, Paige, really. Grandpa was just kidding about Mackenzie the other day. You know, on the staircase. Now let's have our tea in peace," insisted grandma, as she passed a cup of white tiger tea to me, with unsteady hand.

The room fell silent. I was aware of grandma staring at me, then at grandpa and back again. She looked a little pale. I was hurt by my grandparents' indignant attitude towards me. I think I would know if I met two people today. It was not my imagination!

Brad sauntered into the room. Finally, someone I could talk to about what really happened! He smiled at me which always made me feel safe and secure.

"Okay, Mr. O, let's have that chat about tomorrow's list of errands. I picked up your medication for you today. What is Ceoumadin, anyways? The pharmacist said to be careful — only two pills in the evening."

"Bradley, really. It's a blood thinner for Ted's heart," grandma replied.

I noticed my grandparents never seemed to want to talk about grandpa's condition.

"All right, Brad, wheel me into the foyer," grandpa requested.

Our conversation would have to wait. But I wondered what grandpa and Brad needed to talk about in private so much? Then I heard the front door slam shut. I shuddered knowing I would have to suffer through another night alone with my thoughts, or with whomever or whatever visited me in my bedroom the other night... And that realization made me quiver.

CHAPTER NINE

"Grandma, do you think there might be a place for me, in the Manor, to develop some photos?" I asked, as I dried dishes from Hanna's delectable meal of blueberry pancakes.

Mom and grandma sat at the breakfast nook beside the large bay window, overlooking a fountain in the gardens. They looked so cosy.

"Oh, that would be great," mom joined in. "Paige was the school photographer as you know," she said, clearing her throat. "She took fabulous shots at all of the sporting events and extra-curricular activities. It would mean a lot."

Laughing as mom interjected, I realized she still felt she had to speak up for me. I also suspected she was not over the fact that my grandparents and I had stayed in touch.

"Well, I don't know exactly where that should be? I mean what kind of room do you need?" grandma replied, slowly.

"It has to be dark, no windows, must have electricity, and enough room for a makeshift area to hang my pictures for drying. Oh, and it needs lots of ventilation."

"Well, that sounds like a room in the basement," added grandpa, as dad wheeled him into the kitchen. "I'm sure we can fix something up for you! Maybe you'll hang around this Manor a little more often than you have been."

"Thanks a million, grandpa!" I rejoiced noting grandma gave grandpa a side glance; that was odd. My heart raced — I would finally get to take some more photos and perfect my craft. My goal was to enter a Canada-wide photo competition someday.

"By the way, Paige, Bradley dropped in to see you first thing this morning," piped in grandpa. "He said he'll be back after lunch to spend some time with you. I guess his mom is set up on her computer now so she can monitor sales for herself. He won't be needed for awhile."

"Awesome, grandpa," I replied as my cheeks turned red. That was so embarrassing, and, getting old! "Well, I guess I'll go get changed."

"You look great, dear. You're not changing because of Bradley coming over, are you?" asked my mom slyly.

"No, I just feel a little grubby. It's so hot outside — I'm going to wash up. I'll be back to the Manor soon."

I ran out of the Manor before anyone else could get on my case about my motives or appearance. Wow! Do they have to be so obvious about everything they say? Adults! They forget their youth.

It was a particularly sunny day; flowers were in full bloom. There was such an assortment of vibrant colours — from purple and yellow pansies, pink and lavender wildflowers, to beautiful, brilliant, yellow sunflowers and red dogwood bushes. The trees stood still as giants, while birds sang beautifully. I never knew so many cardinals lived in southwestern Ontario. Oddly enough, the male cardinal is the more colourful red and the female is brown with red feathers. Huh! Luckily for us humans, the women outshine the guys!

I counted the steps back to the guest house and should have been near it after one thousand, one hundred and forty two steps. Maybe I was turned around by gazing up so much? I felt panicky, but at the same time, I did not feel alone while trudging along a forgotten path. Okay, I am definitely on the wrong route! The brush was overgrown along the trail, with taller bushes on either side, arching over the path like an inviting gateway. I had to part the underbrush with my feet in order to continue on. It was flatter land, firmer ground than the rocky path I had conquered to the ridge. Flushed, and a bit on edge, I unwittingly stumbled into another adventure. Something unforeseen seemed to push me forward to see what would appear at the end of the path.

Not surprisingly, I felt faint. Don't worry — it will be okay, Paige, I tried to re-assure myself. Then I saw her. She stood probably ten feet high — the most beautiful angel with wings outstretched. She looked gilded, and frozen in time. I was stuck on some lower brush but kicked my way through it. I was so drawn to this statue that once I neared her, I stopped and turned around — I was in the midst of an ancient graveyard. I gave out an involuntary scream. My eyes widened, goose bumps raced across my arms as the hairs stood on end, and I felt chilled. This feeling was all too familiar! Where had I experienced this before? Oh, yes, in the Manor. It was at this point, I keeled over. Next thing I knew, I slowly awakened to a gentle nudge.

"Paige, Paige. Are you all right?" Brad said urgently. "I've been looking for you for two hours. And then, luckily, I heard a faint scream! I figured it must be you. What happened and how on earth did you get over to this part of the estate? It's just over a half a mile from the guest house."

I looked around nervously. "I don't know what happened to be honest, Brad. I thought I was walking to our place and somehow I got off on the wrong path and bam, here I am, on the ground." I rubbed my head; I must have gone down hard.

"Let's get someone to look at you," he insisted, helping me up.

"No, I'm okay, Brad," I replied, dodging his move. "I'd rather my family not find out about this. I feel like I should be here, but they won't agree. They're always so afraid I'm going to hurt myself on this old estate. Overprotective, much?!"

"What could've pulled you here? It's an overgrown, obviously neglected cemetery. I personally find it rather creepy, especially since I didn't even know it existed. I've walked this estate a million times. I'm so lucky to have found you, huh?"

Brad offered his hand again. His eyes were intense.

"It's quite all right, Brad. Look, I'm standing, no one's hurt me. I just felt over-heated. Do you have any water on you?"

"Yeah. I always carry it in the summer. Here you go."

Brad passed me his water bottle from the side pocket of his baggy shorts; his boxers hanging out which always seemed to make me laugh.

"Thank you. Now that we're here, let's look around a bit," I insisted, as I tried to mask my own anxiety.

"That's not such a good idea, Paige. Don't you feel out of place here? Is this your family's private burial ground?"

"Looks like... But my curiousity kicked in. C'mon, where's your sense of adventure? They're dead. No one's gonna bother us here. Besides, there's safety in numbers."

It was so cool to discover this insular setting. It was a small cemetery fenced in on three sides. Clearly, I had walked in on the fourth, open side, which made me wonder — why hadn't it been completely enclosed? There were several tombstones swallowed up by surrounding grasses and weeds; it looked other-worldly.

"Conserve your energy, Paige. You don't want to have another episode," Brad said, rather concerned.

"I am." And as soon as that was said, I tripped. I almost smacked my head on a tomb stone that stood at least a foot above the ground. Since when did I get so clumsy? This was not my day. I turned around to see what entangled my foot. It was some sort of stone engraving, partially buried in the ground. What kind of cemetery has a tablet lying around?

"C'mere, Brad. Look at this," I commanded.

He walked guardedly over to where I was now standing — back at the entrance to this mysterious place.

"What is it?" I queried, hoping to confirm my suspicion.

"Hmm, don't know. I'm not a cemetery specialist. Looks like some words are engraved on it, though."

We looked at it from all angles and still could not make out what it said.

"I think it's some sort of ancient tablet. Perhaps we need to get some cleaner and wipe away the moss and debris. I bet some of my photo chemicals would do it," I said rather cheerily. "My parents are going to buy some for me, in town."

"Photo chemicals? What? Oh, let's just get out of here? Have you seen enough? I'm feeling sick to my stomach."

"Okay, Brad, let's go. I guess that's enough investigating for a while, but I am coming back here, with, or without you, to figure this thing out. Maybe it's a message from one of my ancestors! I mean, how often do you find something like this, from the past? I'm so pumped!"

"Let's go," Brad's voice cracked as he motioned for me to follow him. "I think this is the trail we came in on, Paige. Keep up, okay?"

Unhappy that Brad was not as excited as I was, I quickly forgot about it as I watched him kick through the brush for me. What a chivalrous, cool guy! I did not get to see him enough. We fell silent as we made our way back to the guest house. I sensed Brad's agitation. What was he so spooked about? I'm not. Well, I guess I am a little. This might be the start of something big! Perhaps, a discovery from long ago? How long ago? My thoughts trailed off.

"Okay, Paige, here we are at the path to your place. Let's not forget our way, again, okay?" Brad scolded.

I reflected he might be trying to lighten the mood.

"I want to remember where the path is. Wait a minute and I'll get something to mark it." I ran and grabbed a stone with black, red and greyish flecks. It was quite pretty, actually. "Okay, now we can go."

Brad turned around, shaking his head, "You sure are interesting, Paige. I think life around here just went from zero to a hundred in sixty seconds."

I saw a little twinkle in his eyes and was instantly hot all over. Oh, maybe it's just this July heat.

"C'mon let's grab a pop and cool down. No one told me how humid it would be out in the country," I remarked.

"Hey, this is **not** the country. We aren't all living on farms. It's a village, you know."

"Well, things sure do slow down around here. No one seems to be in a hurry. Not like in Toronto." I shot a smile at Brad. Our friendship had grown and I was grateful for him. His presence was reassuring. What a day it had been! I was surprisingly tired as we arrived at my front door.

"Brad, do you mind if I have a rest? It's been quite the afternoon and they'll be expecting me soon for dinner."

"Sure. No problem Paige. Want to hang out tomorrow after lunch? I'll come by then."

"Great. We'll see what trouble we can get into," I said as I smiled. Thoughts of Mackenzie and Conall popped into my head. It was not the right time to mention them yet!

Brad kissed me gently on the lips. It was so tender. I didn't mind it! I was lost in the moment, until I realized Brad was gone. Wow, could this really be happening? Things are really heating up around here!

CHAPTER TEN

As I lay in bed trying to nap, my mind wandered off to the events of the day and ultimately to the kiss I shared with Brad. I was elated. I never had time for boyfriends because I was so busy back home with tennis and basketball. Both sports kept me running year-round, thanks to the indoor courts at my former high school. And, as the school photographer, I was often called upon last minute to provide my services. My thoughts drifted back to Brad — he sure was handsome in a rather rugged, brawny manner. And when he smiled...and those dark brown eyes... My daydream was rudely interrupted.

"Paige, are you there?" bellowed dad from the front door.

I jumped off the bed, hiding behind my door.

"Paige, where are you?" he hollered.

As dad entered the bedroom, I popped out from my hiding spot.

"Aahhh, Paige! You scared the life out of me! Oh, I get it, from younger days — a bit of the ol' hide n' seek, eh?" dad chuckled.

"Ha, ha. Sorry, Dad. I just couldn't resist. Is it time for dinner?"

"Yes. I came to grab a sweater for your mom. Let's go."

"All right, dad."

We walked along the path together, chatting up a storm. I had always loved my time with dad. He was comical, but, there when I needed him most. Approaching the Manor, I saw another glimmer through one of the second floor windows — a flash of light, a flicker. I chose to dismiss it.

As we entered the drawing room, I was greeted by grandma. "Well, there you are young lady. We've missed you. Your grandfather and I wanted to tell you something. If Grandpa doesn't mind, I'd rather show you in person?"

"Of course, dear, as long as Paige promptly returns to give her dear ol' grandpa a big hug."

"What is it?" I asked. My heart raced a little faster not knowing what to expect.

"This way, Paige. C'mon, follow me."

I looked quizzically at my parents but they gave me nothing.

"Okay Grandma."

We headed towards the kitchen, taking a sharp left before it, down a dark, narrow corridor. I noticed an ever increasing damp smell the farther along we walked. We continued, what seemed forever in silence, until grandma stopped and pulled on a rope chain dangling from the ceiling. 'La voila'- there was light.

"Grandma, where are you taking me?"

"Patience, Paige, you'll see. It's not much farther."

I was just about to say how excited I was, when we arrived upon a three quarter length door. Grandma reached into her right pocket and pulled out what she called — a skeleton key. A skeleton key, what is that? Grandma was mysterious. She delicately inserted the key in the lock and turned it clockwise.

"This is a very special key, Paige, not only for your very own darkroom in the basement, but because it opens any door in this Manor — that's what a skeleton key is," proclaimed grandma, as if she had read my mind. She turned and handed it to me. "Keep it safe in your possession."

"Oh grandma, I'm speechless!" It all seemed so surreal — my own darkroom?! It was at that moment that I really knew I was a part of her family. I gave grandma a heartfelt hug.

"And that's why you haven't seen Dexter lately, or much of your father. They have been renovating the laundry room for you since you moved in. We almost told you yesterday morning when you asked about a studio. It was your Grandpa's idea from the moment we knew you were moving here. Didn't we fool you? Your parents and grandpa were playing along like nothing was happening."

"I don't know what to say." I gave her another hug.

After a moment, grandma let me go and remarked, "Wait until you see it! Now watch yourself walking down these stairs — they take a sharp turn to the right. And don't forget to crouch a bit. They didn't build high basement ceilings back in the day."

"No problem, grandma. I'm right behind you."

The staircase was enclosed on all sides, with light bulbs hung in odd locations along the ceiling illuminating our walk. Like grandma said, a sharp turn to the right and just four more steps down to a cobblestone hallway, ancient in its appearance. It was awesome down here and I loved it! As we marched on, grandma turned into a room on the left. It was three doors past the stairwell and one hundred and eighty six steps from the drawing room. I will have to commit that to memory.

Grandma stopped abruptly, causing me to collide with her.

"Sorry, grandma."

"No, it's my fault, dear. I want you to be the first to enter your photography studio." She backed up and let me go in ahead of her.

"Thanks, grandma," I looked for the light switch and turned it on — I was stunned. It was the studio of my dreams. The ventilation was excellent; I could smell the fresh air.

"Grandma, how can I ever thank you!" I turned and gave her a quick hug. I was so excited to see my new hideaway.

"That's thanks enough, Paige. I cannot take all the credit. I'm going to visit my sister for a few days, and wanted to show you this before I left. Luckily for us, your dad and Dexter had enough knowledge between the two of them on how to renovate this room. And with the list of supplies you gave to your mom, I guess you could say we were all in on it."

"My own photography studio?! This means the world to me," I blurted, as my throat tightened, and, finding it hard to swallow.

"C'mon, then. You promised your grandpa a big hug and I guess everyone else too!" exclaimed grandma.

"Yeah, you're right. Let's go!"

Turning to leave the room, I saw movement in the corner. When I looked back, there was nothing there. I turned off the light and dismissed it. We walked swiftly back to the drawing room.

"Well, Paige, what do you think?" mom asked, as seemingly excited as I was.

I tensed up as all eyes were upon me, and stammered, "I love it — I'm so honoured you all took part in it." Tears welled up in my eyes.

"C'mere, dear. How about a round of hugs for all of us," added my dad, a bit choked up himself.

After hugging my parents whole-heartedly, I walked over to grandpa, beaming, "You really took me by surprise. How can I ever thank you and grandma enough?"

"Well, let's start with that hug," grandpa winked. "We heard you're this big city slicker photographer and now we can see you in action."

I leaned down to hug grandpa in his wheelchair. And as I did, I whispered in his ear, "I'm so very happy we all came back here."

"Me too," grandpa replied gruffly.

"Well now," said Hanna as she entered the room, "I've certainly missed something here, haven't I?

We all laughed in unison as mom confirmed, "What you've just witnessed is the bridging of the generation gap. Mountains have been moved here today."

My mother had no idea just how true that observation was, on so many levels. I could hardly wait to go to bed that night to reflect on this turning point of my 'life in the sticks'. It was so much more exciting than I could ever have dreamed of! One could only imagine what tomorrow would bring?

CHAPTER ELEVEN

Conall scrutinized the room, suspiciously. He wondered what in the world Paige needed with all of this equipment? How difficult could it be to develop some photos? Conall became angry. The more he paced back and forth across the room, the faster the red light in the corridor flickered on and off. It was as if the light alerted visitors to beware.

Conall collapsed onto the floor in the corner to brood, his thumbnail inserted between his two front upper teeth. He was scowling, brows furrowed. It was unforgivable what had been done to his space! Paige had invaded his hideaway. Even Mackenzie did not know where his scheming grounds were located!

* *

Mackenzie wandered the estate in search of her brother. She hoped she would find him, soon! Feeling frustrated, she decided to go and wait at the cottage. Surely, he would eventually turn up there. She wondered what he did by himself, so much.

After what seemed an eternity, she tired and slipped back to the Manor to see if he was spying on the family. Mackenzie quietly crept in through the kitchen door, to peals of laughter. She moved in stealth mode towards the commotion and peeked around the corner. Paige was hugging her grandfather. How nice. But better yet, Mackenzie overheard the conversation about a dark room in the basement. Ah ha. That gave her an idea...

* *

"So this is where you've been hiding all along!" cried Mackenzie. "What are you doing down here?"

Conall reeled around to confront his sister. "If I wanted you to know about my hiding place, I would've told you myself!"

Mackenzie backed away as Conall's eyes burned blood-red in colour. She had never seen him like this. Conall had a mean streak but this reaction was way beyond anything she had ever imagined. Mackenzie started to tremble.

"What are you doing here? Is it because of Paige? Did she tell you? No, how could she? She hasn't met you yet. Well then, how did you find out?" Conall bellowed.

Mackenzie was not just afraid for the O'Brien's, she was now afraid for herself. "I'll come back to see you when you're calmer." She tried to leave, but the door slammed shut and she stood, paralyzed, against her will.

"I'll tell you when you're leaving! I've had it with you trying to follow me around all the time! Come here," Conall commanded.

Mackenzie moved involuntarily across the room. Conall physically overpowered her and threw her into a small closet. She heard the door lock. *How can he do that to me? We have the gift of moving freely on this estate!*

"Conall, let me out of here right now! What are you doing? Have you lost your mind? I'm your sister. Let me out, now!" Mackenzie cried.

Conall stood still and stared menacingly at the door. He shouted, "No, you are going to ruin all of my fun with the O'Brien's! This has been coming on for a long time. No one's going to stop me now, not even you! When it's all over, I'll let you out. And not a minute before."

Conall bolted from the room refusing to listen to Mackenzie's cries for help. He smiled and realized he'd never felt this good in years. *Let the games begin!*

* *

CHAPTER TWELVE

That night, after all of the excitement of the day and the reveal of the new studio, it was impossible to fall asleep. It did not help that the wind howled through the trees outside my window, like something evil encircling the guest house. The branches slammed against the pane as if trying to break into the room. I finally drifted off into a troubled sleep and had the strangest dream about Brad, and his mom, whom I had never met. I could see and hear the two of them so vividly, as an invisible, uninvited guest.

"Why Bradley Adam Parkman, whatever are you thinking?" enquired Sarah with a southern drawl, similar to Scarlett O'Hara's, in the ancient movie Gone with the Wind. She raised her right eyebrow.

"Mom, you're not supposed to sneak up on people like that!" Brad exclaimed.

"It wouldn't be the first time and certainly won't be the last," his mom replied as she giggled.

"Mom?" Brad responded, conveniently changing the subject.

"Yes, dear."

"What is your problem with O'Brien Manor? Even now, when I just mentioned it, you skipped a breath and looked so serious? What are you so afraid of?"

"Nothing, Baps," Sarah stammered.

"C'mon, it's time you told me. I mean it! I've tried to ignore it, but now that Paige is here, it's hard for me. She's a good friend. Should I be worried for her?"

"I don't think so," Sarah hesitated. "I really don't want to talk about it, but if you feel you must know, c'mon and sit down at the kitchen table with me."

"Sure, mom!"

"When I was a young girl, as you know, your Grandma, my mother, cleaned for the O'Brien's. I noticed when she left for work in the mornings, her good mood would disappear and she would look so serious, telling me that someday I would have a career and that I was never to work for the O'Brien family. Being quite young, probably ten years old, I paid no attention to this. Until one day, mom came in the door, returning before her shift was over. She was white as a sheet. I asked her repeatedly what was wrong, but she wouldn't answer me. She simply asked for a glass of water and stared out our kitchen window. So, after a time, I quietly slipped out the back door and left her sitting there. She didn't even notice me leaving. I ran over to the O'Brien Manor and entered through the kitchen door. No one was around. I thought I heard someone talking upstairs so I walked into the foyer and quietly crept up that beautiful winding staircase. When I reached the landing, I heard voices near-by, but couldn't see anyone. Without warning, I felt a hand touch my left shoulder! I ran out of that mansion frantically. I fell down along the path a couple of times before I reached our home. My mom knew as soon as I entered the kitchen, where I had been. She hugged me tightly, so tightly, I thought I was going to suffocate. She made me promise to never enter the Manor again and I haven't. I will keep that promise. Something very unnatural lives in there!"

"Wow, mom, you're really worked up. Why didn't you ever tell me?"

"The O' Brien's have really needed your help and you haven't run across anything unexplainable, have you, Baps?"

"No. I just have this feeling that someone is watching me...sometimes. It's a really creepy feeling! In fact, the first day I met Paige on the path from the Manor to the guest house, I thought I heard voices, two actually — a boy and a girl. They sounded like they were coming up the path and I instinctively hid in the bushes. Moments later, Paige walked up and wondered what the heck I was doing. I didn't want to tell her. I was afraid she'd think I was crazy!"

"That's what I'm talking about! But, somehow I think you are part of the puzzle to help that family. Please keep your eye on them. The O'Brien's are lovely people. I often run in to them in town when Mr. O'Brien has a doctor's appointment. I'm sure Paige is just lovely. When do I get to meet her, Baps?"

"I don't know, mom. Soon... I have to admit — now I'm a lot more concerned for all of them."

"Me too, Baps, me too."

* *

When I awoke early the next morning, I knew I had to see Brad that day! I remembered parts of my dream, but, the details had quickly faded. In no rush to get moving, I happily dropped back to sleep. My last notion was — did I really see Brad and his mom talking about my family, for real?

CHAPTER THIRTEEN

The windstorm had died down from the night before, and I exalted a heavy, sigh of relief from my body. I gradually opened my eyes to catch the morning sun shining brightly through my window, welcoming me to a new day. Leaping out of bed, I quickly dressed in a pair of dark wash, denim shorts and tank top, when my cell phone rang. Thankfully, it was Brad. Coincidence, I was not so sure?

"Good morning, Paige! Do you feel up to visiting that cemetery again?" asked Brad. "I was thinking that maybe you have something there, about that stone tablet. I mean what if it's a message to us?"

"Wow, Brad, that's three-sixty from the other day! You didn't want to get involved. What's changed your mind? Read an inspirational book or something?" I jested.

"Okay, okay. I know I didn't want to believe what you were saying, but I've given it some reflection. Maybe we should investigate the tablet a bit further. And what are we going to do around here anyways? We can only babysit the blue rinse club so much, right?"

"The what?" I responded.

"You know, the blue rinse club. Don't tell me you've never heard of that. Older ladies often tint their silvery hair with a blue rinse. Ladies do it to appear rich but they're just old to me. Hence, the blue rinse club."

"You're crazy, Brad. I'm definitely up for it! I'll grab some chemicals to clean with and water bottles for us. I'll meet you at our stone marker on the path, all right?"

"Sure, give me five. But don't worry about the cleaner, I've got that covered. I asked my mom about cleaning moss off the stone and although she shot me a funny look, she gave me a bio-degradable cleaner that'll do the job. Let's get going on this!"

"Oh, okay. See you soon."

Digging in a cemetery required a completely different outfit. I changed into my treasured sand washed jean shorts and crisp, white t-shirt and my trusty Sketchers. This should be fun! I could not believe Brad had jumped on board about this. Grabbing my cell phone, I tried to silently escape from the guest house, when I spotted my parents enjoying their morning ritual of coffee in the dining room.

"Mom, dad, I'm going out for awhile. See you later." I walked briskly past them hoping to make a clean getaway.

"Wait a minute!" mom called out, as she took a sip.

"Yes, Paige. Tell us, where are you off to now? We thought you'd be in your photo studio all day today," chided dad.

"You guys! You know how much I love it, but I do have to take some pictures first, before I can develop any," I cajoled. I grabbed my camera from the computer desk. "I'm good to go. I'll be taking some awesome nature pics today! This estate is a goldmine of photo ops."

"Okay, then. Grandma and Grandpa want to see you later. You haven't even had breakfast yet!" added mom.

"I'm gonna grab a couple of breakfast bars. You know how filling they are. I'll be fine. And some water. " Reaching into the fridge, I remembered two bottles.

"Hmm, grabbing two, eh? Meeting up with anyone special?" they both teased.

"MYOB, both of you," I shot back. I can't believe the things they come up with. Certainly, they have more to worry about than my social life. I left the house in a huff, face flushed, once again. I was busted.

The stone marker appeared to be missing! I looked around for awhile but the shrubbery seemed to have swallowed it up. I texted Brad and, thankfully, he responded right away. The stone was by the golden rod and red berry bushes. I vaguely remembered where they were. That meant the path must be southwest of our Guest House, if my sense of direction was correct. Thankfully, I knew I was on the right path when I heard Brad singing ahead.

"o're in Killarney, many years ago, me mither sang a song to me, in tones so sweet and low..."

"What song is that?" I interrupted as I walked up behind him. "I've heard it before."

Brad turned around and took my breath away. He was dressed in a navy blue polo shirt with his black jeans and that smile! He had a carpenter's belt on that held the cleaning solution and rags, with a shovel in each hand. He looked steamy! My heart started to pound. I hoped my face didn't reveal my thoughts.

"I'm not sure, Paige. It's something I heard when I was a kid. I'll have to remember to ask my mom, sometime. You look fantastic!"

I returned Brad's smile. "Well then, let's get going. The parental units are on my case today to take some pictures. I'll snap some shots of the stone engravings and maybe we can piece them together, later in the studio?"

"Sounds like a plan. Let me go first. I don't want you to fall like you did last time," Brad said, mischievously.

"After you," I replied, ignoring the sarcasm.

We strolled along in silence as though trying not to disturb anyone. And who exactly was around to disturb out here, anyway? I watched Brad as he politely held the tree branches aside for me, at some challenging spots along the way. My foot got stuck only once. I fell towards Brad and he caught me. He held me close for what seemed minutes, but was merely seconds, and then he gently released me. Brad was intoxicating to be around. I had not felt this way about anyone! We continued along the path. Interestingly enough, this time Brad tripped as he entered the graveyard.

"Ouch!" cried Brad. "Is this where you fell?" He stumbled forward and caught himself.

"I really don't know. What did you get caught on?"

"Looks like we tripped on the same mysterious stone, Paige. Look!"

Brad pulled away the entangled weeds — the tablet was much bigger than we had initially estimated. Together, we worked away to dislodge it.

"Hey, we found a monumental piece of... whatever ," Brad boasted. "You really are onto something, Paige! Help me carry this to the center, over by the angel, and we can look around for other pieces, if there are any?"

We both grunted as Brad picked up one end, and I, the other. It was a lot heavier than it looked. It took us several breaks to move the stone a mere ten feet.

"What does it say?" I gasped, collapsing on a bed of weeds.

"Hard to tell. The moss is embedded in the center of it. I'll try to clean it while you check out the grounds, okay?" Brad said, excitedly.

"Good luck! I hope your cleaner will do the trick. I'm sure your mom knows what she's doing. Give it a try," I said with great anticipation. Maybe we are on to something!

I strolled leisurely, away from Brad, with my head down this time. I did not want to stumble over another thing! The number of graves indicated by small tombstones was overwhelming. They lay strewn around, remembrances from yesteryear, long forgotten. A cool breeze blew across my body, and I realized there was something here beyond our realm. Not wanting to offend whatever, or whoever, it was I walked respectfully over the graves. I looked back at Brad, diligently cleaning the stone, and noticed a flicker of black over his right shoulder. Upon closer observation, I realized something was circling him. I stopped dead in my tracks; my eyes widened. I tried to remain inconspicuous hoping that whatever it was wouldn't come after me! Oh, that's terrible! Looking out for my welfare alone, eh? I quickly snapped out of it.

"Brad, everything okay? What's happening?" I asked urgently.

Brad had not noticed anything out of the ordinary. "It's coming along but I have to use my brute strength. You'll have to use your brain to figure this all out. Get it?" he said, laughing. "You're the brain and I'm the brawn."

I studied him for a moment, confirming the black shadow had disappeared. Interesting! When I spoke, it vanished. I have got to make a mental note of that for next time, if there is a next time.

Turning away from Brad, something pushed me down, forcefully; I was stunned, landing on my elbows and knees and screamed, involuntarily.

Brad ran over to help me. I was trembling as I heard a thundering crash. We both looked back, and were astonished to see that the stone had broken in half. Horrified, I now understood that the black shadow was after the tablet! It did not want us to piece this epitaph together. I blacked out.

"Paige, wake up! What happened?" Brad commanded.

I regained consciousness feeling safe — Brad was clutching me in his arms. It was soothing. I did not want the moment to end.

"Brad, I'm all right." He brushed my hair gently from my face looking so worried. I did not think it was a good idea to tell him what I had seen, just yet. "I think it's the humidity. I'm not used to it. We lived a block from the lake and there was always a breeze, whether it was cool or not. The air here feels so thick — you could cut it with a knife. It sucks the life out of you," I confided.

Brad helped me to my feet. He was such a dream.

"C'mon, Paige. Let's check out the stone!" Brad urged, snapping me back to reality.

I felt rather embarrassed. Focus, Paige, focus!

"Sure, Brad. Right behind you." I felt dazed for a moment, brushing myself off. Then I re-joined Brad. I was thrilled to see most of the words were legible on the stone.

"Did you clean that much of the tablet?" I asked Brad, eagerly.

"No. It must've happened when it split in half. The moss is really hard to get off. But how in the world did it break apart like that? That's what I want to know?!"

"I'm not sure, Brad. Hold on a minute. Can you help me try to piece it back together and then we'll be able to see what it says."

"Okay, Paige. Let's start lifting them on two. One, two!"

We manoeuvred them as close as we could to one another — it was like fitting pieces of a jigsaw puzzle together. I read the profound words to myself:

The mistery which binds me still:
From the torrend, or the fountain,
From the red cliff of the mountain,
From the sun that 'round me roll'd
In its autumn tint of gold –

"Brad? What do you think of this?" I insisted as I pushed him towards the stone.

"I'm reading it!" exclaimed Brad. "Boy, that's foreshadowing isn't it?"

"What do you mean?"

"Well, here we are trying to figure out this mystery. Don't you think 'mistery' with an 'i' means the same thing as 'mystery' with a 'y'? Isn't that what we are doing — trying to solve a mystery?"

"Yeah, I guess we are... I'm sorry, Brad. I guess this has been a bit overwhelming for me. I'm cold and shaky. Whatever happened here today, it's really got me spooked. Mind if we leave?" I did not want to mention to Brad what I had observed. He would never come back here again and maybe it's not what I think at all — it could not be a ghost...

Thankfully, Brad interjected, "Not at all! I really don't know what happened here either, Paige. This is all new territory to me. The graveyard...and I'm cold too, for such a hot day. Let's bounce. We've done enough detective work for today."

"Okay. I'll take a couple of photos, first," I readily agreed.

Once satisfied with the snaps of the tablet, we exited the cemetery and strolled along the path in silence. I took a few more pictures of the surrounding flowers, and of Brad. I could not shake the most dreadful feeling; a feeling of imminent doom. Maybe we had meddled with something we had no business disturbing? Why did I involve Brad in this quest? What had I done?

And then I heard a voice, whisper harshly in my ear, "There's no one to protect you now! Aaahahahahahaha…" A shiver ran down my spine. That ghoulish laugh would haunt me forever!

"Paige? Do you hear that?" Brad said, gruffly. "There's not a sound in the forest. Not even the chatter of the brown squirrel?"

I realized Brad was not aware of the spirit circling us, nor did I want to draw his attention to it, in case it may escalate the situation. I was petrified yet tried to maintain my cool.

"The silence is deafening," I whispered.

It was at this point that the wind picked up and howled through the trees causing branches to whip back and forth. The sky grew dark, thunder crackled, and lightening followed, illuminating the entire forest. A torrential downpour began.

"C'mon, let's bolt! Something's not right," I yelled to Brad above the thunder. "I'm afraid something has happened to my grandpa."

'My grandpa'? Where did that thought come from?

"I'm with ya!" Brad shouted. "Run, Paige, run!"

CHAPTER FOURTEEN

Brad and I darted to the Manor, raced into the kitchen, panting while trying to catch our breath. I faintly overheard my parents and Hanna talking.

"Where's Paige? She should know what's happened," sighed mom. "What does she do on her own so much?"

"C'mere, Miss Lori. Come and sit with me on the couch. It's okay. Please, let's calm down. Paige will show up soon. There's nothing she can do to help at this point. We've got the nurse here watching over your dad — she won't let anything happen to him. Now, I'll go and see if anything is needed, okay?"

"Thanks, Hanna. You're so used to looking after him. It must be hard to give up the reigns."

"Yes, ma'am," retorted Hanna as she left the drawing room.

"I agree with you, Lori. Where is Paige? I don't understand why she's absent so frequently without telling us where she's going. The whole point of coming here was to connect with your folks — for all of us to."

"I don't know what to say, dear. She's a teenager and has found a new friend. She's doing what teens do."

* *

My heart skipped a beat. Brad and I rushed into the drawing room and found my parents seated on the couch, with slumped shoulders, misty eyed and holding hands. "Mom, dad, is everything alright? I've had this terrible premonition that something bad has happened... to Grandpa!"

"Brad. There you are Paige! I don't know an easy way to say this. Your grandpa has slipped into a coma," mom sighed. "He was fine one minute and then he passed out. I couldn't wake him, so your dad called the doctor who's just left. His nurse is staying here in case there's an emergency. Dad's vitals are weak. He's just lying there on his bed, listlessly."

Mom threw herself into dad's arms and cried. Thankfully, he was there to console her. I was more concerned about why grandpa had slipped into a coma.

"Paige, we know you love exploring this place, but we need you here for the time being. You understand, don't you?" implored dad, as he looked sternly at Brad.

"Yes, sir," Brad interjected. "I'll leave now, but if you need anything, anything at all, please call me," Brad volunteered. He turned to leave us in privacy.

"Umm, Brad, could you please stay here and keep Paige company?" mom added.

We need to go into town and pick up a few groceries. Paige needs support right now." She grabbed my dad's hand forcing him to leave the comfort of the couch.

"No problem, Mrs. Maddison. I'd be happy to stay here with Paige, unless you want me to run in to town?"

"No thanks, Brad. We can take care of it. And I'm sure Paige could use your company right now," she suggested.

"Okay, then. Maybe we could play some cards. How about gin rummy, Paige, to take our minds off things?" inquired Brad.

"Gin what? Whatever... sounds good." I smiled, appreciatively, while giving mom the biggest hug. Boy, what she must be going through! This was not how it was supposed to be here.

"Okay then, Lori. Let's go!" dad insisted.

As soon as my parents left the Manor, I had an idea. The basement... Without hesitation, I grabbed Brad's hand. "Let's go to the studio and I can develop my photos from today."

Brad nodded in agreement.

We scrambled down the hall. I unlocked the three quarter length door and we climbed carefully down the stairs. Brad walked ahead of me in the hallway. The lights flickered and the red light for 'studio in use' was flashing. As we approached the doorway, the air became bitterly cold. I broke out into goose bumps from head to toe.

"Brad, something bad is about to happen," I whispered.

"Paige, I'm with you on that. Be careful! Something is just not right. My mom..."

Brad stopped speaking, abruptly. Before we knew it, we were in the studio with a large, black shadow, flitting back and forth. When I looked straight at it, it disappeared, but when I peered at if from a side angle, it seemed almost human in form. I skipped a breath.

"What are you and what are you doing here?!" demanded Brad.

With great force, Brad was tossed out through the doorway like a rag doll, smacking into the opposite wall. He slumped to the floor. I ran out of the studio, slamming the door shut behind me.

"Brad, are you okay? Brad?"

"Ooohhh, that hurt," he replied, writhing in pain. "What was that, Paige? It's not human, that's for sure! What on earth could be haunting us?"

"Haunting us? That's a leap, isn't it, Brad?" I snapped back.

"Oh, c'mon. You feel it too. My mom knows about it. I've felt it since I was a young boy. It's like something's creepin' on this place. My mom told me a story from her childhood. She believes something... else lives in the Manor. She won't even come inside this place. And let's not forget what happened at the cemetery! You didn't think I noticed, eh?"

"I don't know what to say, Brad," I mumbled. "I thought I was going crazy. Many things have happened to me since my arrival. I thought I was losing my mind." I, tenderly, touched his shoulder. "Thanks for sharing that with me. I really thought I was going crazy. I'm even hearing voices."

"Well, are you hearing any now? Because I kinda think we're in trouble if we don't figure this out soon! I'm wondering if this has something to do with your grandpa, like you said earlier."

"I hope not!" I exclaimed.

It was then, that the door to the studio burst open. I was shocked to see Conall standing in the doorway. He had those same goth clothes on. Change your clothes, much?

"Conall, what are you doing here? Did you see that thing in the room?" I cried out.

"Hello, Paige. Who's this? Your boyfriend?" snickered Conall.

"No, he's my friend," I explained. "Brad, this is Conall. I haven't had a chance to talk to you about him, yet."

"Hey, Conall, you must've seen that black shadow... or whatever it was, in the room," Brad stammered.

"No. No one in there but me," Conall replied, grinning from ear to ear. His cheshire-like smile reminded me of the cat in 'Alice in Wonderland'. Then, his face became distorted — his eyes narrowed and turned yellow with a green ring around the irises. It was un-nerving!

I stepped back towards Brad, trying to distance myself from Conall. His human form vanished and he transformed into a monstrous, black apparition that hovered above us.

"How's your grandpa, now, Paige?!" it bellowed. "The ironic thing is that the O'Brien's stole this place from my father, many years ago. Murdoch O'Brien lived in the cottage where you first met me, Paige. Your great, great, grandfather arrived as a guest here from Scotland, mooching off my father, Lyle McDonough, and tricked him at a poker game in front of the townsfolk, to bet this estate on his last hand. My father thought he had won with a full house but Murdoch beat him with four aces. Everyone was horrified but back then a gentleman had to honour his word, or he had no word at all! His reputation as a McDonough would have meant nothing. Let's just say that your relative ran mine off his own property! Lyle McDonough left with his wife and two children. That's right — Mackenzie and me. And, he ended up drinking himself to death. Actually, I think he lived and died in your house, Bradley Adam Parkman."

Brad's face turned ashen.

I was unsure where this conversation was going. The hairs on the back of my neck stood on end and I felt overwhelmingly, nauseous. I was ready to bolt.

"Now, c'mon, Conall, or whoever you are? You aren't going to hold that against us are you? How long ago did that happen? A century? You, you can't still be mad about that, can you?" I stuttered.

'Go into the studio and unlock the closet, now!' I listened to the voice in my head, and swiftly slid past Conall. As luck would have it, he was fixated on Brad. I rushed over to the closet and unlocked the door with my key. Ah, yes, the skeleton key! Mental note — I'll have to thank grandma for that, later. To my surprise, Mackenzie popped out.

"Mackenzie, what on earth...?"

"I'm not sure, Paige... I'm so sorry about Conall. He's lost his mind! But, I'm so glad you're here. Who knows how long I would've been locked up in this dungy, old closet if you hadn't come to rescue me! Thank you, Paige."

"I'm glad to help. But what is going on around here?" I begged.

"Well, if you haven't noticed, Conall and I aren't... human. I guess I have some explaining to do."

"Not now, Mackenzie! Conall has Brad trapped out in the hall! What will he do to him?" I cried.

"He won't hurt your friend, Brad. He's just toying with all of you, for now. I'll make this quick. Let me see, where do I begin? For the first half of the century, things went well for Conall and I. We played together and explored the grounds and the Manor. And then, when your grandfather took over the estate, things began to change. I think it's because your grandpa bears an uncanny resemblance to our father, Lyle McDonough. It was bad enough when father died of alcoholism but then our mother, Anne, died of a broken heart, soon after. At least, that's what the doctors told us. I could see the desperation in my mother's eyes from all the disappointments in her life, but no matter what happened with the loss of the estate, she stuck by our father because she loved him so. To watch your husband drink himself to death was more than she could bear. Conall adored our mother. He worshipped the ground she walked on. I think the rage inside him stayed dormant until your grandpa ruled the estate. Okay, enough of that! Paige, I think you and Brad had better leave now! I will try to distract Conall. Let's go," Mackenzie whispered. She led me out into the hall.

"Conall, why are you torturing these people? What have they ever done to you? We were living here peacefully, and now this? What happened?!" Mackenzie demanded.

Mercifully, Brad had passed out. The shadow moved towards me, then hastily retreated to Mackenzie. Then poof, Conall was back in the flesh. As Mackenzie and Conall began to argue, I nudged Brad awake and grasped his hand to escape. We fled upstairs and down the hall to the kitchen and out through the back door.

"Paige, what is going on?" Brad said, choking. "I'm so freaked out right now. I don't even know what just happened, do you?"

"I wanted to tell you about Mackenzie and Conall, Brad, but I thought I had imagined them. I met them soon after we moved here and was very troubled by it, but I couldn't bring myself to talk about it... with anyone," I slowly replied. "Well, actually I did mention meeting them to my grandparents, and they acted like I was crazy — like I made them up. I don't know what Conall and Mackenzie are doing here, or how they're even here? I've never believed in the spiritual world, but then again, I've never had any experience with death. I can hardly believe we're talking about this. Is this for real?"

"Paige, we'd better get on board with this. I didn't throw myself against the wall and I have bruises to show for it. Look at my right side," Brad exclaimed as he pulled up his shirt, and exposed a black and blue, baseball-sized bruise.

"Oh, no. I'm so sorry! I feel like it's all my fault. I should've said something sooner," I sobbed.

"No, I wouldn't have believed you, if you did. Some things you just have to see for yourself," Brad said, consolingly.

We stopped talking for a moment and listened to the rainfall beating down on the overhang above us, on the outdoor patio. It was just as frightening outside in the elements, as it was in the basement. I moved closer to Brad, as he put his arm around me. There was nothing we could do but listen to the comforting sound of our breath, in and out. Brad turned me towards him and we had a passionate kiss. It was much more meaningful in the midst of all of this craziness. We embraced for a while longer until Brad whispered, "Paige, I'd better go and see what else I can find out from my mother. I'll be back later to see how things are. In the meantime, don't go back to the basement and make sure you're with someone at all times!" Brad ordered.

"Fine, but what about you?"

"I don't really think Conall is after me. I think he wants to mess with your family — your grandfather, in particular. Maybe my mom knows something. I'll call you."

"Bye, Brad. Come back soon," I said faintly.

I watched Brad sprint down the path and felt a sudden surge of protectiveness run through me. If that Conall does anything to harm him, he'll have to answer to me!

I walked back into the kitchen and felt surprisingly secure. Is that what a kiss can do for you? I looked around hesitantly and was happy not to see any sign of Mackenzie or Conall. They must be having it out downstairs. I hastened to grandpa's bedroom to watch over him.

"Hanna, how is grandpa doing?" I asked, upon entering his room.

"Paige, I'm so glad to see you. Come here and sit on the bed. Your grandpa will know you're here, whether he can tell you himself, or not," Hanna said, graciously.

I smiled at her. Hanna had such a wise face but really was not that old upon closer observation, maybe mid fifties? Judging by the number of wrinkles around her hazel eyes and mouth, I came to the conclusion she had not had an easy life. She was a bit plumpish but what did that matter? She never took a sick day according to my grandma and had a heart of gold; a hearty soul. It was evident she was happy living here with my grandparents, but what of her past? I put aside my curiosity and watched as Hanna purposefully wiped grandpa's forehead, with a cool cloth. Perhaps she was testing him to see if he would react to a physical sensation? Clearly, Hanna adored him.

"Hanna, would you like me to take over?" I suggested.

"No, dear. It's quite all right. I've been doing this for years. I wouldn't feel like I was doing my job as his caregiver if I didn't look after him."

"I understand. I guess my parents will be back soon?"

The nurse appeared and interrupted our tranquil moment, announcing we should leave the room while she turned grandpa on his side for some relief from his backside. I agreed to leave the room while Hanna insisted she would assist with this task. I stopped and looked back at grandpa from the doorway, and noticed a black shadow suspended over his bed. Oh, no! It was Conall in my room that night when mom barged in and interrupted him! It's his doing after all! He's hurting grandpa! Now what can I do to save him?

And with a strength inside I never knew I had, I became enraged and knew the answer to this other-worldly predicament was mine to be had! The word, tablet, popped into my head. The tables have turned now, Conall! I'm not going to let you hurt another person. I hope you are ready to rumble!

CHAPTER FIFTEEN

My parents returned from their trip to town more subdued than ever. Mom's face looked drawn and the twinkle in my dad's eyes had vanished. I was sure the gravity of the situation had hit them hard. It had only been a short time since we arrived, and we were already closer to my grandparents. What an unfortunate time for this to happen to them, and for grandma, while she was off visiting with her sister! What a shock this will be when she gets back!

Hanna had encouraged my parents to keep quiet about grandpa's situation until grandma returned. After all, she had looked after grandpa each day, every day, as much as she could. His needs were so great, Hanna pointed out that she was hired to help, and Brad was asked to run errands. I could not imagine what it must have been like for grandma all those years; looking after an ailing husband, and alienated from your only daughter and her family- I felt choked up. I silently begged the universal intelligence — let it not create a rift in this family, ever again, please!

"Paige, how would you like to go back to the guest house with me and let your mom have some time with her father?" dad suggested.

"Sure, dad. I can understand why mom needs to be with grandpa. Luckily, they forgave each other before this happened... I've had quite the day myself," I acknowledged. I knew we were doing the right thing for mom, and could not wait to get back home to devise a plan to help grandpa.

"Okay, Lori. Paige and I will see you later. Don't stay too late. Remember — Hanna has looked after your dad very well for the past several years," dad offered, gently. "And the nurse is here."

"Yes, dear, I know. I'll see you both later." Mom smiled, weakly, blowing us both a kiss.

"Thank goodness your grandma has a selection of umbrellas for a stormy day like this one, Paige, or we'd be soaked before we started!" dad teased, as he pulled a rainbow coloured umbrella from the stand by the kitchen door.

I paused for a moment before answering him. His face looked sincere when he called the Guest House, 'home'. The twinkle in his baby blue eyes was back. Although tall, he was small-boned and slim, with refined features on his tanned, wrinkle-free face which contrasted handsomely with his blond hair. He loved the outdoors. Mom and I often teased him about how much food he could pack away in one meal, without gaining a pound. We, on the other hand, only needed to look at food, and then, if we didn't exercise.... What a horrible thought!

"Home, yes it does feel like home, Dad. And I agree. Grandma's very thoughtful. I hope she's enjoying her time away. It'll be tough on her when she gets back."

"You never know, dear. Your grandpa may awaken from his coma at any time. The doctor could not provide any sound medical reason for it. His vitals are almost normal. Maybe a little weak in the heart, but he's a tough ol' guy."

"Yeah, he is. In the short time I've known him, I've found that he soldiers on without a complaint."

"You got that right. Now, enough of that. Are you ready to make a run for it? Try to stay under the umbrella, okay?"

"I'll try to keep up," I cajoled.

We both laughed as we bolted from the Manor. We ran seven hundred and twenty three steps to the guest house. Dad quickly unlocked the mammoth wooden door and flung it open. We burst into the house, breathless. I happened to look up at the ceiling. The angels did not look like they were flying anymore. In fact, they looked still and sombre. I quickly looked away. I did not need any more negative imagery in my head tonight.

"Dad? I think I'll go to bed."

"Okay, dear. Get a good night's sleep. We don't know what's in store for us tomorrow. Mom will need to lean on both of us." And with that comment, he hugged me good night.

Tossing and turning in bed, I believed that with such a comfortable mattress and cosy duvet, surely sleep would overcome me.

Apparently not! The events of the day raced through my mind. After an hour of restlessness, I turned the table lamp on and noticed my backpack strewn on the floor, with two books peeking out. And then it hit me — the books from the library in Conall's dilapidated cottage! I had forgotten about them. I crept over to retrieve the books and remembered they were covered in dust. Grabbing an old t-shirt, I proceeded to gently brush the dust off the cover of one, and in doing so, made the second book drop off the bed, landing with a thump. It fell open to a poem that caught my eye. The word 'mistery' shone like a beacon. My eyes could not believe what they were seeing, and my heart palpitated. Maybe this is the key to all the trouble in O'Brien Manor?

Unfortunately, it was then I hit the 'wall'. My energy dipped, the urge to resolve the problem slipped away as I gave in to the exhaustion from the day. I would have to wait until morning to play the saviour.

CHAPTER SIXTEEN

Waking early, the annoying sunshine streamed through the window, again! I would have to remember to close my curtains, next time! I texted Brad to come over as soon as possible. He messaged he'd be right over. I got up and called for dad, but my voice eerily echoed through-out an empty guest house. He must have returned to the Manor. Mom had not come home, by the looks of their unmade bed. It would never have been left so messy. My heart pounded and I painfully realized maybe something bad had happened to grandpa. I calmed myself down and refocused. If instincts were trustworthy, mine were telling me all was well. Surely dad would have roused me to accompany him to the Manor, if grandpa's condition had deterio-rated. I quickly changed just in time for an impatient knock at the front door, and ran to greet my new boyfriend. Whoops — did I just think that?

"Hi Brad. You'll never guess what I found," I blurted out, opening the door.

"Well, you'll never guess what I found out," he mimicked.

"You, first."

"No, Paige, you go first. You're the one who invited me over."

"I found the poem, the one that has 'mistery which binds' in it. Can you believe it?" I boasted, arms outstretched.

"You're kidding me! Let me see it."

"Sure, I'll go grab it from my room."

When I returned, Brad had positioned himself on the loveseat in the hallway and was motioning me to sit down. Reaching out for the book, he said, "Mind if I read it out loud?"

I smiled at his suggestion, "Absolutely — please, go ahead."

ALONE
From childhood's hour I have not been
As others were — I have not seen
As others saw — I could not bring
My passions from a common spring.
From the same source I have not taken
My sorrow; I could not awaken
My heart to joy at the same tone;
And all I lov'd, I lov'd alone.
Then — in my childhood — in the dawn
Of a most stormy life — was drawn
From ev'ry depth of good and ill
The mistery which binds me still:
From the torrend, or the fountain,
From the red cliff of the mountain,
From the sun that 'round me roll'd
In its autumn tint of gold –
From the lightening in the sky
As it pass'd me flying by –
From the thunder and the storm,
And the cloud that took the form
(When the rest of Heaven was blue)
Of a demon in my view.
Edgar Allan Poe (1809-1849)

"Wow, this is heavy," I remarked. "What does it mean? A demon! Is someone speaking of death, an evil spirit, or what? It's pretty dark, don't you agree, Brad?"

"Yeah, it's certainly about death, or demons, or something like that, but what is its significance? Why is this poem carved on stone in your cemetery? That is — assuming the rest of the broken tablet pieces finish the verses off."

"Maybe Mackenzie can help us? I'll have to seek her out today. First things, first, though. I need to check on my grandpa. Will you come with me? Then we can decide what to do from there?"

"Sure, Paige. That's just too weird you found the actual poem. Or at least it seems to be."

"I'm not so sure I found it, Brad. I was cleaning off the cover of one of the books I took from Conall's cottage, when the other book fell to the ground and popped open to this very page. Did I find it, or did someone help me?" I mused. "Wait a minute, what were you going to tell me?"

"Oh, it can wait. It's not as newsworthy as this. Let's get to the Manor."

We walked hand in hand, listening to the blue jays' screech and the cardinals' high pitched chirps. The critters of the forest were coming to life. It was a cloudless, sunny day, in stark contrast to last night's wicked storm. Tree limbs and leaves were strewn about. Yet, all seemed to point to a good omen of peaceful days to come. Brad strolled ahead and opened the kitchen door for me. I beamed as I walked by him. Somehow, along this journey, Brad and I had become more than friends. Life can be pretty amazing!

"Good morning, Paige, Brad," mom welcomed, as we entered grandpa's room. "So glad to see you here, so early. Hanna's making breakfast for us. Would you two join us?"

"That would be wonderful, mom."

Brad rubbed his stomach in agreement.

"How's grandpa today?"

"He seems to be stabilized. I'm hoping he'll come out of this soon. Your grandma will be home tomorrow. She will be devastated and angry at all of us for not contacting her and letting her know. Just be prepared. I hope, eventually, she'll understand we wanted to give her a break."

"Mom, it'll all be okay. Grandma needed some time with her sister and we've been handling things here at home." I hugged her dearly.

"C'mon everyone," Hanna said, as she walked in on the conversation. She studied mom for a moment. "Let's enjoy our breakfast. I made your grandpa's favourite, in his honour. Maybe he'll wake up to the smell of good ol' porridge and a wee bit of brown sugar and strawberries. That's the way he always liked it. Oh, tell me I didn't say 'liked'. I mean he likes it," Hanna corrected herself. We could see she was horrified at her mistake, as she grimaced and bowed her head.

"It's okay, Hanna. We're all uneasy. I'm going to stay with Ted," dad insisted. "You guys go and have your breakfast and then I'll have mine. I don't want to leave your dad alone, Lori."

Mom attempted to lighten the mood, "Okay, dear. But don't tell him any of your racy jokes. Hey, maybe you should. That'll wake him up for sure."

We left the room and sat around the dining room table. Everyone was silent. The sunlight shone through the windows framing the front foyer. It was so good to see something positive. This will be the day to remember, as I figure out that tablet, with Brad's help, of course!

"Thanks, Hanna, for a great start. You make the best porridge in the county. Is there anything I can do for you?" Brad enquired.

"No thank you, Brad. You're doing quite enough, entertaining Paige. I'm glad you two get along so well."

Mom was listening intently to Hanna. She had a glazed look in her eyes. I guess she does remember her teen years, after all. That, or she's exhausted.

"Well, now, Paige," dad bellowed from the other room. "There's not much you can do here this morning, so why don't you develop your photos of the other day. We could all use some cheering up. They're nature pics, aren't they?"

"Yeah. Sure, dad. Brad, maybe you could come and assist?" I proposed.

"Sure, Paige. Whatever you need — I'm your guy," Brad chuckled, eyes twinkling.

"Okay with you, mom?"

"Absolutely, dear. You two go ahead. We'll be fine. There are more than enough of us to watch over grandpa," she said assuredly.

"Great. C'mon Brad. Let's get to it," I bounced out of the room.

As soon as we were out of earshot, I turned to Brad and asked, "Are we sure we want to go back down to the basement? I have the chills just thinking about it."

"I know. Me, too! What I wanted to tell you the other day was that the original owner of the O'Brien Manor lost this estate in a card game and ended up living in my house. Your front stone archway used to read McDonough Manor, not O'Brien. How weird is that? My mom told me."

"I know. Mackenzie told me. Not only did he move to your house, he died there, and his wife too! He became an alcoholic. His wife died of a broken heart, or so they say. How sad is that? I think that part of the history of this estate is somehow tied into what's happening to all of us now, and especially to my grandpa. Mackenzie told me Conall has a vendetta against grandpa and the O'Brien's because of that infamous night."

"Well, I can understand to some extent. Is that why they've come back? It must be his rage keeping him here, and Mackenzie's insistence on accompanying Conall in his wallowing. Like any good, little sister would do."

"We need to figure out how to put Conall to rest. Mackenzie will follow," I suggested.

"How do we do that?"

"I think I've got a solution. We need to find the missing pieces of the tablet and put them back together. I noticed in the cemetery, that the more you cleaned the tablet, the larger, and blacker Conall's shadow grew. He is threatened by whatever that tablet signifies."

"Wait, a minute. You mean it was Conall there in the cemetery! He broke the tablet?" yelled Brad. "I knew something weird was happening but not that!"

"I didn't want to alarm you the other day, Brad. I hope you understand."

"Looking back on it, I do. I would have been out of my mind," Brad acknowledged, thankfully.

"Okay. Let's hit the cemetery. I'm glad you stashed your work-belt by the path the other day, so we can get down to business. We're going to figure this thing out for my grandpa's sake, before it's too late."

And with that consideration, we hurried to the path, grabbed the belt and dashed along the path to the cemetery. I was winded. It was visible Brad was too. We stood silently for a few minutes surveying the scene.

"Brad, we found the first piece as we entered the cemetery on the open side. Let's look at the mid-point of the other three borders and see if any pieces are buried there."

"Why there?" Brad responded.

"I don't know. Just a hunch," I muttered as I looked up at the direction of the angel's outstretched arm. "Here's a shovel. I'll take the fence on the right and maybe you can dig near the fence opposite to the entrance. I'll use this smaller shovel to dig. Hurry, Brad."

We had both worked for about half an hour when I hit something hard, about six inches beneath the surface. I checked to see if there was any sign of Conall and, with relief, glanced up at the angel. With the sun behind her — it appeared as if she was pointing in the opposite direction.

"Brad, could you stop digging where you are and start over there on the other side of the angel, please? Hurry!"

"What's up, Paige?"

"I don't know, please, just go over where the angel is pointing and start digging, fast!" I said urgently.

I did not want to announce aloud that I had located a piece of the tablet nor my reasons for the urgency; I sensed Conall would show up soon. Brad dug as quickly as he could, as did I. I uncovered a bigger piece of the tablet with six lines carved into it. At that same moment, Brad hit something so hard, the sound echoed throughout the forest.

"Hurry, Brad. Please get it uncovered already," I uttered in a harsh tone.

"Okay, okay, Paige. I'm dying here. This is breaking my back, but for your grandfather and you, I would do anything," he replied, then paused. "Paige. Come over here. You've got to see this."

I dropped my shovel and sprinted over to Brad. There in the ground was a small piece of the tablet. Brad carefully brushed off the dirt. It read –

From childhood's hour I have not been,
As other's were; I have not seen,
As others saw; I could not bring,
My passions from a common spring.
From the same source I have not taken

We silently laboured and swiftly moved the tablet over to the angel.

"Do you think Conall carved this?" I conjectured. "It's someone writing about their unsettled childhood. I wonder how old Conall was, and Mackenzie, when their parents died?"

"I was ten, and my brother was seventeen — about your age, Paige," answered Mackenzie. "I've come here to warn you. Conall's on his way. He's responsible for your grandpa's illness. But he's been alerted to the fact that you two are here. Run!"

Before we darted from the graveyard, I tossed dirt on the tablet I had unearthed. I did not want Conall to see just how close we were to revealing his secret. I camouflaged our supplies, as well, with tree branches. We sped down the path until we heard a voice ahead. Both Brad and I hopped into the shrubs to hide.

"Wait'll the O'Brien's see what I've got planned for them next! They won't believe it! When I'm finished with Ted, I'll hurt the grandma and after that, the new family. Vengeance is sweet. Who said otherwise?" Conall muttered.

The tree branches and shrubs shook as Conall stormed by. I held my breath as he paused to look around, before continuing on. I found it curious. He was back in human form. I was thrilled he was not around grandpa. Any time he wasn't near him, grandpa's chances of survival increased.

I whispered to Brad, "Let's stay here awhile. Conall doesn't know where we are and I really want to get back and finish what we started. We are so close to solving the mystery."

Brad looked long and hard at me, before answering. "Paige, I don't want anything to happen to you. You heard Conall. He's coming after all of you."

"I'll be fine, Brad. I don't have any other choice. I'm not going to rest until I help my family. Are you with me on this?"

"Of course," Brad surrendered.

We fell silent. It was incredible that such a beautiful day could serve as the backdrop for so much turmoil and evil. I knew deep within my heart that we were very close to resolving the puzzle. Surely, Conall wanted to be at peace. No one could enjoy such evil acts, and the torture of innocent people. He must have been shattered by the loss of his parents. Wait a minute. That's it! The poem. He carved it on the tablet while mourning his parents' death! It talks about a lonely childhood. His parents were preoccupied with their woes, they probably did not spend much time with their kids. That's why he and Mackenzie were so close. We have got to finish the restoration of that tablet!

"I think the coast is clear now, Brad. Let's go back to the cemetery to finish this job once and for all."

Brad bounded up in agreement. We hurried along the path but were shocked to find Conall still in the cemetery. Brad shoved me under the bushes, in the nick of time. Conall was pacing back and forth in front of the angel. He was talking to someone, but who it was — we had no idea. Conall was a character you did not want to stare at for too long. I had the shakes just watching him. He was engrossed in his own little world. Who could he be talking to? Does he have a co-conspirator? To my surprise, he dropped to his knees and raised his fists over head.

"I miss you so much, mother. Why did all of this have to happen? We had such a good life together, the four of us. I hate the O'Brien's for what they've done! They took my family away from me. I will never forgive them for that! Never!"

With that admission, Conall — up and disappeared. Brad and I made no move. I was afraid Conall would come back or was hiding. Brad seemed to be as terrified as I was. Finally, Brad stood up and motioned to me to follow him into the cemetery.

"How do you know Conall is gone?" I whispered.

"I just know, Paige. His offensive smell has dissipated."

"What are you talking about?" I laughed, thankful to relieve some tension.

"You know — it's like a bad egg or something.... Quit teasing me. Now let's get to work! I think Conall's headed to the Manor, which isn't a good thing for your grandfather."

"You're right."

I hastily uncovered my piece of the tablet. I waved Brad over. We hoisted it up and moved it next to the angel, beside our original discovery. The tablet read:

My sorrow; I could not awaken
My heart to joy at the same tone;
And all I loved, I loved alone.
Then — in my childhood, in the dawn
Of a most stormy life — was drawn
From every depth of good and ill

I knew in my soul, time was running out. My chest tightened and my breathing became laboured. I looked around, anxiously, to see if Conall was watching us from the shadows, and was relieved there seemed to be no sign of him. The longer I stood near the angel, the more I felt this reassurance that all would be well. I studied her. She looked different from the last time we were here. Could she be coming to life? Did I just think that? Then that recurring sickly feeling returned; only slightly different.

"Brad, Brad! We have to get back to my grandfather! Something terrible is happening. I can feel it. Let's go, now!" I screamed hysterically.

"Okay, Paige. I'm with you! Let's run like the wind."

Brad's long legs took him far ahead of me. I was so grateful to have a good friend like him. He was so trusting and supportive. As we approached the Manor, a huge, black, swirling cloud rose above it. It was like someone was stirring a pot of extreme evil. I knew this would not be good.

Brad burst into the kitchen. I stumbled in next. Hanna was standing there; her face white. My heart sank.

"Hanna, is grandpa, okay?" I shouted, bursting into tears.

"Oh, Paige. Thank goodness you two are back! Your grandpa has slipped into a deeper coma. The doctor's not sure if he'll ever come out of it. I'm so sorry, dear," Hanna trembled.

"Where are my parents?" I commanded. Without awaiting an answer, I dashed to grandpa's side. Mom was crying with her head down on grandpa's bed, holding his hand. Dad was standing with his hand resting on mom's shoulder. It looked as if they had been in that position for quite awhile; statues paying homage to a great man!

"Dad, can I have some time with mom and grandpa?" I asked quietly.

He seemed to be in a trance. There was a delay before dad replied, "Go ahead, Paige. We don't know how much longer Grandpa has." He kissed my forehead lightly as he left the room.

Dad stopped in the hallway and spoke to Brad, in hushed tones. I could not hear a word they were saying and quickly became frustrated! Mom didn't even notice me. I placed my hand on her shoulder and whispered in her ear, "I love you, mom. I'm so sorry about grandpa."

Mom did not respond; it was as if she was in a trance, too. I knew who was at the bottom of this and I felt the same rage I had experienced last night. How dare Conall think he can get away with this! I backed out of the room and snuck by Brad and dad. They had moved to the dining room and were so engrossed in their conversation; they were not even aware of my presence. It was then that I accepted that the last part of the battle was mine to resolve!

I stealthfully navigated my way along the path, turning right to the cemetery. I knew I was taking a chance going alone, but somehow I knew the angel was there to protect me. My fear had subsided. I did not remember much of the trek there being so highly distracted. The bigger shovel was under the brush right where Brad had placed it. I grabbed it and walked over to the remaining section of fence, digging with all my might into the adjacent ground. Splintering pain ran through my hand, and up my arm, across my shoulder and over the top of my head. I was in agony. Somehow, I managed a smile. Hopefully, I had hit upon the last piece of the puzzle. Now we'll see who's winning the battle!

Everything moved in slow motion. Each time I dug into the earth, dirt flew high into the air around me. The smell of the soil was almost unbearable. It permeated my nose as I imagined a person being buried alive. I was having an out of body experience watching myself, this teenage girl, fighting with determination, to uncover the 'mistery' once and for all. I brushed the soil off the tablet and recited the last few phrases of the puzzle:

From the lightning in the sky
As it pass'd me flying by –
From the thunder and the storm,
And the cloud that took the form
When the rest of Heaven was blue
Of a demon in my view.

Snatching the shovel, I wedged it under the tablet, and pushed the stone upwards, and onto its side, wondering how it was I did not break my back. I then manoeuvred the stone up and onto the ground. How would I ever get it over to the angel? I dropped onto the forsaken ground for a rest. I can figure this out?! My favourite Kanye West song popped into my head. I sang 'N-n-now th-that don't kill me, can only make me stronger, I need you to hurry up now 'Cause I can't wait much longer. That's how long I've been on ya. I need ya right now, I need you right now'. And with that truly inspirational lyric from Stronger in mind, I had a vision of mom, crying over her dad, as he lied there, helplessly. I rose up and with the aid of the shovel, propped the tablet on it and began to push it towards the statue. Wherever my strength came from, I would never understand it, or question it. After quite a struggle, I finished re-assembling the pieces. I was elated — like the time I put my first difficult Harry Potter puzzle together. However, this was the ultimate jigsaw puzzle! Lying in front of me, was the complete poem from Conall's dusty, old book. I was fixated on the last line — 'A demon in my view'. The lone sound of my heart beat was the last thing I remembered before losing consciousness.

* *

CHAPTER SEVENTEEN

I lay peacefully in the cemetery, dreaming, awaking in a semi-conscious state.

Mackenzie bent down and placed her hands gently on my temples. I could not move, nor respond to her, yet felt light as a feather as I floated up and out of my body guided and transported to the Manor. I observed my family and Brad from a distant place.

"Miss Lori, your mother's home! Her taxi just pulled in the drive. Miss Lori? Kevin, could you please tell Miss Lori her mother's here?" Hanna hollered as she peeked out between the curtains in the front window.

Brad walked up behind Hanna and put his hands on her shoulders, "Hanna, I'll let her know," he said kindly. He tread quietly into grandpa's bedroom.

"Mrs. Maddison?" Brad whispered, and when mom did not respond, he looked over to my dad, disconcertedly.

"It's okay, Brad. We heard Hanna," dad responded. "Lori, you must go to the door to tell your mother. She'll be devastated! I agree with Hanna. The news should come from you."

"All right, then! Will you and Brad please stay here with dad while I'm gone?" snapped mom.

"Sure thing, Mrs. M," Brad quickly agreed. Dad nodded at Brad to join him by grandpa's bedside.

"Your mom is almost in the door, Miss Lori. What are you going to tell her?" asked Hanna, as mom entered the foyer.

"The truth, Hanna. There's nothing else to say." Mom opened the door to welcome grandma. "Hi mom, we're so glad you're home. I have some news, some... very unfortunate news..."

"Well, dear, can it wait until I at least get my bags inside? Where is everyone? I thought your husband might help me with my bags, not you, dear."

"Umm, he's busy right now. Sorry, mom. Anyway, I need to tell you..."

"Really, Lori. Can't it wait? I've just had a long trip home and I'm tired. I want to see your dad. Where is he?"

"That's what I need to talk to you about. There's no easy way to say this."

"Say what, dear? Come on. Spit it out!"

"Dad's fallen into a coma. It happened the day after you left. I'm so sorry."

"What! Why didn't you call me? I would have come right home. Take me to him now!"

They both charged into the bedroom. Hanna followed, as she wiped her hands over and over again on her apron.

"Kevin, what's the matter with Ted? What happened to my husband?"

"I'm so sorry, Helen. The doctor doesn't know why this happened. Ted seemed fine when you left but became a bit dizzy. I helped him to bed. When I checked in on him, he was unresponsive. The doctor is baffled but Ted is stable. He was in a mild coma, but regrettably, he's slipped into a deeper one," explained dad, as sensitively as he could.

"Now, you listen here, Ted. This is your wife speaking and I'll have none of this. Are you trying to punish me for going away for a few days? What? What is this?"

"Mom, please calm down. We've been taking good care of him. Hanna has been here around the clock, with the nurse, and the doctor is checking on dad each day."

"Calm down? Calm down!? How exactly do you expect me to do that? I go away for a few days and I come home to this?" Grandma's Scottish accent had returned. She waved her arms about in frustration.

"C'mon now, Mrs. O'Brien. Let me make you a cup of my green tea and we'll all sit down and talk calmer around Mr. O'Brien, okay?" Hanna offered as she reached out to take her by the hand.

"Okay, Hanna. You're always the yardstick of common sense around here."

I spied Conall observing my family, and for one intense moment, saw into his wicked mind; his warped thoughts. I woke up with a start, covered in sweat. For a moment, I didn't know where I was, until a vulture swooped towards me and then flew away!

* *

CHAPTER EIGHTEEN

This is pretty cool! Look at all those O'Brien's having a fit about their precious Ted. I haven't had this much fun, ever! The look of desperation on all of their faces. It's delicious! Especially the grandma. Boy, is she shocked! I hope she's really feeling it. And that daughter, Lori. What did she expect? She left this place and her parents to fend for themselves. I would never have left my parents' side! I would have done anything for them! Now they can feel the pain of losing someone they love so much — a parent. I will never get over the loss of my mother or my father! Their deaths occurred, one after the other. It was this family that brought shame on mine and caused our destruction!

I feed off their anguish. It only makes me stronger. Boy, I wish Paige could see them now. Wait a minute. Paige? Where is she? Her boyfriend's here. Every time I'm having some fun, she goes missing! I will not let her mess this up for me! Oh, no. She's not going to mess this up! Hey grandpa Ted, I'll be back...

* *

CHAPTER NINETEEN

I revelled in my accomplishment — I had successfully completed the puzzle! Fear was no longer in my repertoire. In my heart, a sense of love and overall peaceful serenity took hold. I knew when Conall was coming — the hairs on the back of my neck stood on end. But this time, there was an acuity, an awareness, that I had never experienced before. I felt fully alive and powerful!

I smiled up at the ever-present angel and watched in disbelief, as she transformed into a beautiful, floating angel that hovered gracefully in the sky above me. She had the most serene expression on her face, her long hair blowing delicately in the wind. Her white dress flowed back and forth as if dancing to slow, rhythmic music I could not comprehend. I knew in that moment everything was going to be okay, or so I hoped.

A black shadow glided swiftly towards me and, then, quickly backed off. It kept advancing and retreating. I sighed with relief. It was as if the angel had built a force field around me. I watched with anticipation to see how the two beings would interact. The angel hovered near me, smiling as if there wasn't a worry in the world. Maybe there isn't in her world, but in mine, it was a different story. It seemed to continue for hours, until finally, Conall appeared in human form with a puzzled look on his face.

"Conall, my son," the angel bellowed, "why are you still here walking this earth? What happened to you, my dear?"

"Mother, is that you?" he cried out.

"Yes, my dear child. It is me. It seems as if someone has awoken me from my peaceful slumber and I'm assuming that someone is Paige, here."

"I re-connected the pieces of the tablet, that had the poem Alone etched on them. Immediately, it grew intensely bright and melded together as one. It was mystifying!" I interjected; half apologetically.

"No worries, child. After I died, my son carved that tablet with a hammer and a chisel to commemorate my death, I believe. He laid it at the foot of my tombstone."

"That is so, mother. I was distraught over the loss of you and father. But, three days later, after it was completed... in a fit of rage, I shattered it and buried the pieces. I became bitter in my heart after the shock of losing both you and father. A day after that episode, I encouraged Mackenzie to come with me to explore the old cottage. In order to get there, we had to navigate our way to the ridge and down that precarious, steep slope. You know... the one with the many jagged rocks. I was so reckless that day! Mackenzie slipped from my hands, as I was helping her down the hill. She was only ten years old when she died, mother. I was devastated and in a fit of rage, lost my footing and fell to my death, too. We've been wandering these grounds ever since that day, searching for you and father."

"Oh, my dear son! How tragic! I'm so sorry that happened to the two of you after I died! You were both left alone with no one to protect you. I am so sorry, Conall," his mother replied softly. "But why, dear child, have you been terrorizing the O'Brien's?"

"You know why, mother. They are the very reason father lost this estate in that ludicrous poker game, so many years ago."

"Is that the way you remember it? My child..."

"Isn't that the truth?" Conall interrupted his mother.

"No, that isn't exactly what happened, Conall. Your father had a gambling problem and owed the O'Brien's a lot of money. Murdoch O'Brien was an honourable man and let the debt go unpaid for many years. But, when they became destitute, we took them in at the cottage. It was then that your dad and I both decided to give Murdoch, and his family, this estate in repayment. We felt we were to blame — the catalyst to their financial ruin! The only way Murdoch would accept this sizeable gift was to win it in a poker game. Your father knew what he was doing. He intended to lose the estate to Murdoch that night. Any injury to our family after that, was ours and ours alone. It had nothing to do with the O'Brien's."

Conall fell silent as he slumped to the ground. Mackenzie materialized, looked up at her mother, and instantly collapsed.

"Oh, mother! How I've missed you so. Can it really be you?" Mackenzie cried.

"Yes, my dear daughter. I've missed you both for so long. Thankfully, Conall, because of the increased intensity of your despair, and the restoration of the tablet, I was permitted to come back to this good earth. Please come and join me in peace and leave this poor family be. Conall, I command you to break the hold on Paige's grandfather! This family is innocent! I do not want another McDonough causing harm to the O'Briens!" his mother trumpeted.

Conall disappeared and returned within minutes.

"Paige, I owe you and your family a world of apologies. I am so sorry for all the harm that I have done. I hope you can forgive me, someday," Conall pleaded.

"I will as long as my grandfather's okay," I stammered.

"You may want to go and see him, now," Conall suggested, as he lowered his head.

Conall and Mackenzie changed forms, one last time, to angels. I gasped, as their porcelain-like faces reminded me of the dolls mom used to play with up in the attic. Could it have been Mackenzie and Conall? The serenity of their faces pushed that question out of my mind. Their mother clutched their hands and turned to smile at me.

"We are sorry for all the pain and sorrow we have caused you, and your family," she said softly. "Forgive us, please?!"

And, as I arose to give my answer, Conall, Mackenzie and their Mother disappeared in the blink of an eye! The Manor, yes Paige, time to get back to the Manor! I was overwhelmingly elated and could not wait to see my family, and Brad. This 'mistery' was over!

EPILOGUE

I studiously observed my grandfather, from the dining room. He was standing in the kitchen, drying dishes for my grandmother. It was still so hard to believe — not only did my grandfather snap out of the coma, he was walking again! After many rigorous tests, the doctors could not explain his miraculous recovery. I smiled to myself. Oh, but I could! Would anyone ever believe me? Nope. My explanation for this medical mystery was that the longer Conall's spirit existed, the stronger, and more evil he became, thereby, affecting the health of my grandfather. He grew weaker and weaker until finally ending up in a coma where Conall trapped his soul, indefinitely. What a purely wicked being Conall was! Thankfully, when his mother appeared, all of his defences weakened and Conall returned to his innocent youth and soft nature. I could not help but notice the pure love he had for his mother and his family. It was truly heart warming to see! It was exactly what I shared with my family.

It had been two months since we moved to the Estate. And I loved it! I could not believe the change in me — the confidence and feeling of belonging within my soul. There was nothing more empowering to me than having helped my family, knowing I was the only one who could. Soon school would be starting and I looked forward to the challenges to come. Brad had decided to pursue a career in architecture. Although I was happy for him, I missed him each and every day. We kept in constant touch by texts.

I slipped quietly down to my studio where I spent most of my days, now. I did not experience any more chills or thrills. There were no more spirits haunting us. I was secure in my being.

I began to develop the photos from the start of my adventure at O'Brien Manor. It seemed like years ago. The pictures of the tablets were somewhat blurred, which surprised me. I have a steady hand. When I developed the photos of Brad walking along the path back to the Manor, I noticed two images surrounding him. One was a white shadow, the other was black. Well, it was not too difficult to figure out who they were. Obviously, Mackenzie was the pure soul, hence white, and the evil soul, Conall, was the black shadow. It was reassuring that the events that had transpired this summer, were not all in my head. They were captured forever in the photos.

A few weeks after my grandfather was feeling better, and we realized he could walk, I set up a photo shoot. Hanna, my parents, my grandparents, Brad and yes, I finally met his mother — Sarah, and Dexter, gathered for the picture. I set up my tripod so we could all be immortalized on film. I was so anxious to develop this particular photo.

Initially, the photo looked like a big blur. My heart fluttered. As it remained immersed in the chemical bath, however, everyone eventually came into clear view. I carefully hung the photo to dry. Hmmm — something just didn't seem right? I held it under the spotlight and scrutinized the photo. Grabbing my magnifying glass, I spotted the problem and that queasy feeling sank to the pit of my stomach. The air turned freezing cold and goose bumps raged from head to toe. Oh no! This cannot be happening! I realized, horrifically, that Dexter's image was not reflected in the picture. I dropped to my knees as I crumpled the photo. What now?! *Sacrilege!*

About the Author

Photo by Cole Bennett

Lee Bice-Matheson is the first time author of *Wake Me Up Inside*, the first in a trilogy. She has narratives published in *The Big Book of Canadian Hauntings*, John Robert Colombo, c2009, entitled Two Experiences. Lee is passionate about the subject of ghosts and hearing other people's ghost stories! She lives with her husband and best friend, Kevin, and their Havanese pup, Kobi, in Orillia, Canada, while their wonderful, loving son, Justin, attends McGill University. You can find her online at leebicematheson.ca, Facebook, Youtube and Twitter (BiceMatheson). Lee has degrees in Honors History, Master of Library & Information Science, The University of Western Ontario. She has worked in public, medical, and corporate libraries, and now works proudly with her husband, in his Chiropractic Clinic.